WHAT IS SAID ABOUT ELEPHANTS

Stories

Wendell Mayo

For information contact:
Unsolicited Press
Portland, Oregon
www.unsolicitedpress.com
orders@unsolicitedpress.com
619-354-8005

Cover Design: Kathryn Gerhardt
Editor: Caitlin James
ISBN: 978-1-950730-55-1

ACKNOWLEDGMENTS

"What Is Said About Elephants" first appeared in *Vestal Review*, "When the Moon Was Ours for the Taking" in *Event*, "A Mindfulness Becoming Less" in *Confrontation*, "The Ponce de León Senior Therapy Swim" in *Slush Pile*, "La Lengua Serpentina" in *The Journal*, "Vigil for *Ammospiza nigréscens*" in *The Little Magazine,* "Two Dimes" in *The Ledge Poetry and Fiction Magazine*, "The Hermitage, 2:10 P.M." in *Westview,* "His Mother, from a Great Distance" in *Zone 3*, "Burn Barrel" in *Lake Effect*, "Heating and Cooling People" in *The Heartlands Today,* "Darnel's Garden" in *South Dakota Review*, and "The Saddest Story He Ever Tells" (as "Hands") in *Masque & Spectacle*, Additionally, the author thanks *CutBank* for including "When the Moon Was Ours for the Taking" in a limited-edition chapbook.

CONTENTS

FOREWORD

Wendell Mayo: Words of the Master

When I first received the news of Wendell Mayo's passing, I found I could not immediately process it. There was his picture on my BGSU Facebook feed, and I presumed he'd just been awarded another in a very long line of accolades.

Then I saw the headline.

And yet I did not immediately believe it. Wendell seemed eternal, a constant fixture at Bowling Green State University, where a great many writers cut their teeth under his tutelage, including a future Pulitzer Prize winner, several indy-press bestsellers, and later, one of my own undergraduate students. He was there when I arrived, and when I visited my girlfriend (now wife) who was still attending the graduate program, and when I came to promote my first book, a copy of which I proudly placed in his hands. In fact, just this morning I was thinking I'd bring him a copy of *Feral Boy Meets Girl*, out from this very press, the next time I visited Bowling Green.

And then, just as quickly, I remembered.

When I think of him, I remember a collection of little things: his dry sense of humor, which could provoke a guilty laugh at unexpected moments. The pocket tees he wore to class, always navy or black, with jeans frayed at the legs from his beaten-up sneakers. The genuine smile that overtook his whole face when he read a passage he enjoyed in class, or when he read something that was truly great. The belly laugh that rocked his whole body. I remember him taking oranges out of his briefcase before class, peeling them, separating all the wedges and sharing them with us, just because. Conferences in a local coffee shop because he was fond of the chocolate-filled croissants they served there. His commonly-used expression, "It's your life," which he typically said after a disagreement over a line or scene we insisted on keeping, but which also meant he respected our creative choices.

And there are bigger things as well. His great love of Lithuania and its culture—he visited many times and frequently taught there in summer, and based much of his work on its history and culture. That he walked away from a six-figure job as a chemical engineer to earn his MFA and doctorate and write and teach, because those were his passions. His quiet devotion to Debbie, his wife and best friend. It was easy to see that when you saw them together. His pride in his daughters, Amy and Jennifer.

Of course, many of us in the literary community knew Wendell as teacher and mentor, first at IUPU-Layfayette, then the university of Louisiana at Lafayette, and finally at Bowling Green State University, and his importance as teacher and mentor cannot be overstated. Wendell was, as a teacher, largely invested in letting us do our own thing, then making it work in the best way we could, both globally and down to the sentence level. His classes were intense experiences in which we were all held accountable for the feedback we gave—Wendell expected equal evidence for a critique or effusive praise—with the understanding that this would make us better readers and, as a consequence, better writers. The most important thing I took away from the experience was to take ownership of my writing in a way I had never done before—Wendell treated stories, even bad ones (a few of which may have been submitted by me), not simply as academic exercises, but rather as works of art that could, and should, evolve and have a life beyond the confines of a fiction workshop. He spoke not of contracts and royalties (though he did teach us about those things), but of the pure art of writing—it was the craft that mattered most. At a dark time when the many complications of personal and professional life threatened to derail me, he calmly advised me, "Writing well is the best revenge." He was right then, as now.

Wendell's legacy endures not only in his own books, but also in the dozens of books, and hundreds of short stories, published by his students over the years: the dark, yet playful tone; sentences that fall like hammer blows; the importance of a good beginning (he once made us promise not to begin stories with characters waking up to an alarm clock); allowing stories to escalate to their logical (or illogical) extremes; the absolute necessity of having a strong ending image or line that sticks with the reader long after they've finished the story; the rhythm and flow of a perfect sentence. You'll see that here as well—Wendell's writing is perhaps the purest form of that aesthetic.

Before I left BGSU to teach composition at a remote two-year college in southwest Indiana, I thanked him for all he'd done for me. He simply replied, "Pass it on." I've certainly tried. As a teacher of creative writing myself, I've tried to pass on the same knowledge and love of craft that he imparted to me. He is always my first and best model of what a teacher ought to be, and it's my hope that, in thirteen years of teaching fiction writing, I've been a Wendell to someone else.

Wendell was a short story writer. That was the form he loved. He didn't care about writing big-box literary novels, and he eschewed the idea of writing as big business. A true artist working in rarified form, Wendell was fully dedicated to the craft itself. His stories were never done— he once told us he continued to revise them even after they'd been collected in book form. This was revelatory to twenty-four-year-old me: young, impatient, wanting to be done with a story and move on. Luckily for us, he's left us with six prior volumes of short stories to revisit, or to discover him for the first time: *Centaur of the North*; his novel-in-stories *In Lithuanian Wood*, translated into Lithuanian as *Vilko valanda; B. Horror*; his chapbook *When The Moon Was Ours For The Taking*, collected here; *The Cucumber King of Kedainiai*; and *Survival House*. He was a master of the novel-in-stories, weaving disparate tales together into a coherent whole, yet allowing each story to stand on its own. While the subject matter may be disparate—cold-war anxiety, Lithuanian culture and legends, family narratives that may or may not be true, the many ways in which horror manifests itself in everyday life—Wendell's stories are highly imaginative, driven by a bemused darkness that makes palatable even the most unpleasant truths and lends an aura of unease to the most benign moments. Wendell's use of language also shines through the many stories he's left us: the short, terse sentence that stabs like an ice pick, exploding into small fits of lyricism; the openings that are darkly funny and profoundly sad at the same time; the sense of imbalance and unease they create; the simple, direct declarative statements pared to maximum potency, with no wasted words or florid prose to clutter their meaning. His long list of awards and accolades stand as testaments to his obvious commitment to his art form, and anyone who knew him and his work also knew those accolades were well-deserved.

Though it's been over a year, it's still difficult to write these things in the past tense, and I'm resisting the urge to go back and fix it. I take some small comfort that Wendell's legacy endures, so in a sense, I don't have to.

Wendell leaves behind a family who loved him, plus a significant community of writers who are better and stronger practitioners of their craft because of his tutelage. A collection of his works and papers in the Bowling Green State University's Jerome Library's Center For The Short Story, which he was key in establishing. Over a hundred published short stories in journals and magazines; and his collections of short stories, all of which are still available for lovers of short fiction to discover and become entranced. And this collection, the final work of a master storyteller and teacher—one more chance to become transfixed, to be unsettled, to smile that uncomfortable smile his work so often provokes, and to learn from him— ever the master, ever the teacher.

I can't wait.

William Jablonsky
Dubuque, Iowa
August 2020

WHAT IS SAID ABOUT ELEPHANTS

BECAUSE YOU PROMISED Soledad many times to go with her to the zoo, but never went, you visit her elephants, using the senior discount card she'd gotten for you both, though she'd only used it once, before liver dialysis, jaundice eyes; before her passing on.

Now a cold, ocherous morning sky follows you, all the way to the Tembo Trail, where, alone, you lean on the icy railing, not sure the elephants will be out, though evidence abounds: elephant snot and mud-smeared Plexiglas, the scent of elephant dung that makes you woozy. But there's no sign of them, just mounds of sand, and three tall telephone poles rising out the frozen ground, fitted with steel I-beams resembling ribs of an umbrella, over which a dense, khaki netting is fastened, dimly reminiscent of fever trees of the Savannah, their dusty yellow bark, stark silhouettes against a saffron sky, a young Soledad at your side. Alive.

You hardly have time to choke back rising grief, to push away from the rail and start home, when Beasley, the trainer—so it says on his nametag—leans in at your elbow like a walking stick, waiting, as young people sometimes wait, for recognition.

"I don't see any elephants," you grumble with bilious disinterest.

Beasley leaves, mercifully. Again, you push from the rail to go home, then notice on your right a hole in a stucco portion of the barrier, a feeding portal, a hinged wire screen covering it. You hear the rumble of elephant steps stopping on just the other side. You look through the portal, can just make out the mountainous slope of the animal's derrière and its tail whipping back and forth.

Then Beasley reappears, right at your elbow.

"There you go, mister," he says. "Meet Victoria."

You hear Victoria swat her side of the portal with her trunk like a major-leaguer.

"How can I meet her if I can't really see her?" you ask.

"Right." Beasley smiles. "Come, Vickie!"

Victoria lumbers into full side view, just inches behind the Plexiglas, too much to take in all at once, so you fix your gaze on her tiny yellow eye at the vortex of her gray, wrinkled sea of swirling flesh, rippled folds of skin that draw you inward, to a yellow center in which there is no memory of Soledad's jaundice, only a pulsing in your neck, the vaguest sound of Victoria snuffling at frozen ground, a swish of air, a throb like distant thunder, fever trees, sounds muttered more than meant, the color yellow, and no other yellow before the everlasting yellow in the eye of the elephant.

14

"It's said," Beasley says, "an elephant won't pass by a dead elephant without casting a branch or some dust on the body. A kind of homage, I suppose."

You turn to Beasley.

"Kid," you say, "what else can you tell me about elephants?"

WHEN THE MOON WAS OURS FOR THE TAKING

THERE'S NO PHOTOGRAPHIC evidence we ever made the trip.

Still, I can picture you: May 1967, a pale afternoon Moon in the sky, the way its ghost hangs overhead reminding me it's always there. You're snapping new car-top carriers onto chrome strips of our Ford Galaxie. A red-and-white fishing spoon hangs just above your ear, planted in your khaki ball cap by one barb of its treble hook. The other two barbs dangle, dangerously exposed.

Mom calls to you through the screen door facing the driveway and Galaxie.

"About ready for your penance?"

"Penance?" I say and look at you.

"Think guilt—penitentiary," she replies. "Your father's doing his time."

You smile, launch our tent and sleeping gear onto the Galaxie, then jerk the load into place between the carriers, your way of punctuating your silent response to Mom. That January, Apollo I's Grissom, White, and Chaffee lost their lives in a capsule fire. There's a race to the Moon. A man who works for NASA can't possibly spend enough time with his family. So the fishing trip is to make up for all the nights and weekends you've not been home.

Still, despite your wearing the deep-green, two-pockets rayon shirt you say you "rescued" from the 1950s, I can't take the science out of you: white pocket protector snug on your left breast, "Property of U.S. Government" gray click-pen poking out, your black horn-rimmed glasses, the crew cut, with a smear of butch wax creating a miniscule ski-launch jutting over your forehead. You wear stovepipe black slacks and the latest in experimental space-age footwear, Corfam plastic oxfords. We have matching pairs. *Not* my idea.

I guess your not being around much isn't all bad. There's less chance of getting in trouble, like a kid whose dad works with you at NASA. The kid accidentally set fire to the woods behind their apartments and his father belt-whipped him, left this scar, like a tiny crater between the kid's eyes where the belt buckle caught him. Kid wasn't supposed to turn around.

I'd overheard you and Mom.

"It wasn't Tripp Archer, was it?" Mom asked. "His son's only three."

You lowered your head as if paying for the sins of all fathers using belts on their kids.

"No," you mumbled, "it's a new guy, fresh up from Houston. Brilliant scientist, actually."

"Yeah, brilliant," Mom said.

You've never whipped me—doubt you have it in you—but when I'm about ready to get into trouble, Mom'll stick a finger between my eyes, my imaginary Moon-crater, and say, "Remember," ominously, then, "your father will be home sometime."

I don't know much about a trip to the Moon, only that we're taking our Galaxie from Cleveland, and we're headed far north to Canada. You've made me complete my schoolwork a week early so we can go.

After school lets out for summer, other kids are going to Cedar Point or as far as Disneyland.

They asked me, "Where you going?"

"Canada," I replied.

One kid said, "They got any good rides there?"

My guess is that you're paid to think about such adventurous distances. The CIA said you could tell us this much: you work on getting us to the Moon—and beyond—"The farther the better," you said, so I assume the farther *north* the better, all the way to Temagami, way north of Toronto, way *north* of *North* Bay.

You tug at the tongue of our trailer and new fourteen-foot boat you've christened *Meteor* with—what else? —a Mercury outboard.

"Fishing's better the farther north we go," you say.

We've never been north of Cleveland Hopkins International Airport.

I take hold of the tongue as well, and we walk the trailer and boat to the Galaxie, where you drop the tongue onto the hitch and stomp it in place.

"Well, then," I say, "let's just go all the way to the North Pole. Bound to be some whoppers there."

You glance at me through your horn-rims, mumble something, then arch your right eyebrow, what seems to be a funny imitation of Mr. Spock in the new TV series *Star Trek*. I almost laugh, then remember you've never seen a second of the show, say you hear at NASA there are too many scientific inaccuracies. So Mom and I sneak down to the basement to catch the show on the old Westinghouse.

Mom comes through the side screen door, stands next to me. She's heard my crack about the North Pole, sticks a finger on my forehead, says, "Remember, wise guy. We're going fishing for your father's sake, to assuage *his* guilt."

"Assuage?" I say.

She winks at me, knowing you can hear us. "Like put a *Band-Aid* on it."

Most everything I know about the English language I know thanks to my Earthling mother, not my half-Vulcan father.

You cinch a canvas tarp over the Galaxie's lump of camping supplies.

Mom says, "Get that silly fishing lure out of your hat," and you remove the cap, pull open the door to the Galaxie, and toss it in the glove box.

"Now, everyone get to bed," you say.

It's still blazing afternoon and, to an ordinary Earthling, it may seem strange that we will wake at two a.m. and launch ourselves north.

"To avoid traffic," you'd said when you sprung the plan on Mom.

"Avoid?" Mom said. "It's more like driving in *a void*!"

Nonetheless, my theory is that you must like dark, empty highways. They remind you of outer space.

So Mom and I are both in a dreamlike sleepwalk when you fetch us at two a.m. and lead us to the Galaxie, reminding me of your mother's account of being abducted by an alien in 1953.

I groggily look into the night sky and swear I see the Man in NASA's Moon laughing at me. Then you pack me into the back seat.

When I come around, the first thing I see is a sign:

ONTARIO IN ITS SECOND CENTURY
1967 to 2067

It is only after consulting my equally sleepy, but still verbally capable, Earth mother that I realize we have not jumped in time to the year 2067.

We round Toronto and rocket north on Highway 11. I watch the speedometer climb, like you've been away from your home world so long you're in a hurry to get back. You stop at a service station with a brontosaurus hovering over pumps. Inside, you exchange U.S. dollars for Canadian.

Back in the car, Mom says, "Look how weird the money is."

We fly along, see signs that say QEW and OPP.

"You're not in Ohio anymore," you say, voice Wizard-of-Ozish, Spock eye arching in the rearview mirror.

I start to play with the strange currency, a bill with Queen Elizabeth II on it, hold it out the window where it flaps in the breeze.

Mom glances at you, then me, says, "Stop it. It's not play money," but I can tell she only says it for your sake.

I scoot across the back seat to avoid your gaze in the rearview.

"I can see everything you do back there," you warn, a reference to your claim that you've equipped your horn-rims with special invisible wide-angle, backward-looking mirrors.

I almost believe you and take to watching the new world race by.

I suppose if one were to be abducted by a space alien, there comes a point when being afraid gives over to a sense of wonder. The highway narrows and mounts a land of massive boulders, blue, green, gray granite splotched with pale green and mustard lichen. Pines shorten and crowd one another in forests thick as carpet pile, some growing straight out of mossy patches on boulders. Small blue lakes rush past my window, some with dark soggy trunks of dying pines poking out of the shallows. Other lakes are dotted with boulders, their submerged bottoms vanishing into blue-black water of unimaginable depth.

I can see Mom's eyes are full of wonder, too.

"Stop," she tells you. "Let's get a picture."

The Galaxie slows and pulls to the side of the road.

You have this look, both eyebrows up, wide-eyed, like Spock gets when he can't explain some mystery of outer space to Kirk.

"I can't believe I forgot the Polaroid," you say.

Mom says nothing, gets this whisper of a smile, like she's satisfied your fallible human half is still there.

We accelerate again, north. More road signs zip by, with words like Ojibwa, Algonquin, Wanapitei. I mumble aloud "Temagami" and you say, "Ojibwa means 'land of deep water,'" like you've lived there before.

Five hours after we shoot north from Toronto, you slow, turning left at a sign:

MARTEN RIVER PROVINCIAL PARK

A wooden, otter-like creature rests its forepaws on the M.

The road bends, crosses a bridge, then disappears into a thick forest.

"People actually camp here?" I say.

"Your father knows what he's doing," Mom says.

But I'm not so sure when the park ranger who registers us says, "You're a bit early this time of year, but technically, we *are* open."

We drive to our campsite, passing only two small tents in the hundred-plus spots. We find out Canadians think we're "hardcore" when you stop at one site for directions. A young man, wearing a winter jacket, warns us we'll encounter mosquitoes like B-29s, blackflies like spitfires, and nights so cold he encourages us to "Hang in there."

But when we reach our site, a rocky, pine-needle-strewn affair, you're prepared. You break out our winter jackets and distribute them to us like a quartermaster, set six citronella candles flickering in the northern breeze, pat OFF on yourself like aftershave, then hand the stinking stuff to me, then to Mom, who wonders, "Will it ever come OFF?"

Mom's batting at pesky insects like King Kong swatting airplanes atop the Empire State Building, then she races off with a bucket to fetch some water from a hand pump nearby.

I help you set up the mosquito netting and tent. Tables and chairs are out of the question. "Our couch," you say, and roll a log over to the cold, ashen fire pit, then set the propane cook stove on a stump and the Coleman cooler next to it. Just as Mom returns with our water, you retrieve our foodstuffs from the Galaxie, place them in your old Navy duffle, tie one end of a rope to the buckle, a rock to the other end, and launch it over a pine branch.

You hoist our food high.

Mom and I stare at our provisions dangling over our heads.

"Don't worry," you say, "it's just so bears and wolves won't get it."

Mom drops the bucket. It lands flat, but water sloshes out.

"And you let me fetch water by myself?"

"Oh, heck," you reply, "bears and wolves are probably more afraid of *you*."

"Probably?" Mom huffs, stomps off to our tree stump, and sets a pot to boil.

I join you on our couch-log. You spread a map across our knees.

"Marten River's really a lake, not a river," you say, then retrieve the government pen from your shirt pocket and draw a black line over a red one, labeled, "Original River Channel, 90 Feet." A blue line runs outside the red line, then yellow, and green. You concentrate on the map, calculating something. Your jaws set and temples beat when your pure logic kicks in. You rifle through a breast pocket, retrieve a piece of paper with columns—"Time of Year," "Species," and "Depth"—your temples pulsing faster, until you tap the map with the pen, and declare, "Fish are forty feet deep, right here."

Mom hands you a cup of hot coffee. Little clouds of steam rise from it.

"All right, Izaac Walton," she says. "Genius angler. When I fetched your water, the man we talked to coming in said, 'Pickerel under the highway bridge with minnows and jigs, and pike farther out in Laroche Bay in lily pads with spoons.'"

I live for moments like this, when my Earthling mother uses common sense to correct the spaceman. It gives me a kind of faith in humanity, that we will survive the atomic bomb and space race, that somehow, we might prevent you from drifting away into deep space forever. I glance upward, cannot find the daylight ghost Moon, and for a moment feel reassured.

The rest of the day and evening we spend in our mosquito tent watching the insect airshow. That evening, in my sleeping bag, vapor from my breath rising to meet yours and Mom's, I keep thinking how any moment a bear, frustrated that you've hung our food high in a tree, might tear the tent open and come for us.

In the morning, Mom's got a wad of canned bacon in the frying pan, and you invite her to go fishing.

"No thanks," she says. "I'm good. It's your mission."

After breakfast, we carry the *Meteor* to shore and launch it in a lake spread with wisps of mist under a blue sky. A loon calls, alternating between laughing and a soft, mournful howl. Tall pines cut a sawtooth silhouette in the dawn sky. You tilt the *Meteor*'s prop into the lake, prime it, pull the cord, and it sputters to life with a little cough of smoke.

As we pull out into the lake, the *Meteor* is the solitary disturbance in the clear, deep water, a single point of boiling, from which our wake, a perfect vee, spreads slowly ashore and laps at boulders. It's lonely and scary, but for the first time since beginning our trip, I look at you and think, if anyone can see us through this strange land, you can.

On the way out, you pull the *Meteor* into another dinosaur fuel stop and pick up some minnows. When we arrive under the highway bridge, you plop the anchor overboard, we bait up, drop our lines in the water, and wait.

And wait.

I've plenty of time to inspect my new rod and reel, to think back on how, when you could get a break from NASA, we practiced casting in our snow-filled backyard in Cleveland, how we studied *Field and Stream* like pros.

"I got forty-pound test monofilament line in the reels," you say. "It'll take a real monster to break that line."

But monsters are not interested. We pull up our jigs baited with minnows, see the small dead fish, spongy and waterlogged.

"No pickerel's gonna eat that," you say.

After drowning a dozen more minnows between us, you reach into the back of the *Meteor* and reveal the fishing cap stabbed with the red-and-white spoon. You tear the fabric a little, removing the barb and hook, and hand the lure to me.

"Young people have all the luck," you say. "Let's go after those northern pike."

We motor out to Laroche Bay and anchor in a stand of lily pads.

"Cast out from the pads," you instruct. "Otherwise, you'll snag."

You snap a black-and-white spoon on your line, cast out, and I follow with the lucky red-and-white. Again and again, I watch our spoons wobble and flash in the clear water as we crank them in.

After an hour, you remove your torn cap, scratch your head, say, "Heck, if I were a pike, I'd snatch one of those dazzling spoons right away."

You sound like a stage announcer trying to buy time until the main act arrives, smiling all the while with a brave face. A moment I'm overwhelmed by your bringing us all this distance, following your penitent dream, but I know when we return to Cleveland, your sights will be back on the Moon.

The way it happens is science fiction: first, a great green fin breaking surface, Godzilla lurking beneath, then the monster exploding into view with my spoon jangling in its mouth.

You toss your rod into the bottom of the boat and grab the net. Your hands shake. My rod's bent double, half of it underwater.

You repeat what we read in *Field and Stream*: "Set the hook, but not too much force! Take your time!"

Easier said than done since the monster rises and begins to orbit the *Meteor*. I rotate on my butt to follow the creature, but it accelerates, twisting the forty-pound line around you, so busy cheering me on you forget to duck. Once, twice, at least a half-dozen times, the pike circles the *Meteor* and wraps the line around you. At last, the monster jumps, gives us a toothy pike grin, splashes back down, and snags the line at the bottom. In the end, we see the monster's fin cutting a proud path back to deeper water.

You look at your bindings, the taut line snagged at the bottom, the other end through the top guide of my rod. You nod at the new fishing knife we ordered from *Field and Stream*.

"Son, cut me loose," you say.

I start for the knife, then rock back and reseat myself.

"Knife's right there," you say, puzzlement spreading over your face, Spock-eyed.

I'm not sure what comes over me. Maybe it's losing the monster. Maybe I don't want to lose anything else.

"I got you now," I say. "You're not going anywhere, spaceman!"

You roll your eyes skyward, and I'm thinking you're calling your mothership in orbit for help.

"I get it," you smile, laughing. "I'm guilty as charged."

I wait with the eternal patience of the fisherman.

"Now, cut me free."

I wait.

"No, seriously, son!"

* * *

FATHER, I CUT the line from you that day, filament by filament.

And when you were free, I feared you might fly up and remain a speck on the laughing face of the afternoon Moon—and you didn't, at least for a while.

When you and I returned fishless, Mom came over and sat next to me on the log-couch by the campfire. I told her the story of how I'd captured you on Laroche Bay. She gently pressed a finger to my forehead, and whispered, "Remember," that time not a warning, but a reminder to not forget.

Later that evening, I watched sparks from our campfire sail up to the Moon. You and Mom looked up at the night sky so long I thought your necks might lock in place.

"The Moon's right there for the taking," you said.

Who would have guessed that only two years later we would take the Moon, and, later within the lifetimes of you and Mom, choose to not return?

I know what you might think of me, so many years later writing down events of our first and last adventure far-north, as if they are happening now. Not one photograph to rely on. Writing, writing. Line by line. Filament by filament. Only now trying to understand your love of distant places.

You might say I've built a rocket fast enough to travel back in time to relive those moments. You might say, "How implausible. How terribly unscientific."

And you'd be right.

I have my penance, too.

These days, I'm no longer interested in the Moon's vast Sea of Tranquility, the historic spot the Eagle touched down. I don't explore the Moon's greater oceans of rock and dust.

Instead, I chart its lesser bodies.

Lucas Solitudinis...Lake of Solitude

Lucas Temporis...Lake of Time

Lucas Sonorium...Lake of Dreams

Each of these reminds me of some ancient, milder calamity, each crater formed by a smaller meteor, our *Meteor*, coming from an unimaginable distance, each a memento of that moment I thought I had you right where I wanted you, each a chance collision of matter in a far-off place.

A MINDFULNESS
BECOMING LESS

AFTER EIGHTY-TWO DAYS without work, Homer Lynch decided he didn't need anything, not his lousy job at Global Vibes in Cleveland testing cell phones, not the separation pay they offered him in exchange for training his replacement in Zhongshan, China, not the COBRA health insurance, the insipid black-eyed snake that ran over two grand a month. And there was more, plenty he didn't need. He only had to think and more would've come to him, if not for a brief lapse of memory, experienced all at once, standing in boxers, at midnight, furnace sighing at the end of its cycle.

He looked ahead to see his way clear to the end of the mustard-lit hallway, then to the kitchen, trying to remember. He thought back to Soledad in their bed, the woman he'd married thirty-eight years before, snoring softly, pillows piled between them like concrete dividers he'd seen construction crews use. But when he made it to the kitchen, he forgot why he came, the reason he'd come out of their bed, out of his dream of Corpus Christi and the 1911 Springfield his uncle Conrad had given him on his thirteenth birthday.

"Just remember, boy," Conrad said and handed him the rifle. He leaned over one hip and spat tobacco juice near Homer's boot. "Be damned careful. This weapon is more than a rifle. It can make an end of things."

Conrad was partly right. The Springfield was more than a rifle. Homer remembered Texas brush-holly and prickled knees, callous-wrinkled elbows scrabbling in the dust, waiting for deer. But Conrad was wrong, too. To Homer, the Springfield was more than the end of things. It was all moments before the ends of things, aligning the sights, dribbling breath over his lower lip as he slowly squeezed the trigger, the painful kick of the stock in the pit of his arm, the rush of smoke out the barrel. The buck going to both knees. The smell. It wasn't sport. They needed the venison. When he was only two years old, Great Depression years, his father left Corpus, left his mother, left him, left everyone to look for work in California, to send money back, only he'd gone for good and never sent anything back.

The fridge door made a little smooching sound when he peeled it open.

A piece of roast venison sat in pale light.

Now he remembered.

He reached for it.

"What are you doing up?"

Soledad's voice. Right at his ear like a little conscience-creature perched on his shoulder.

"I'm hungry," he growled. "I want a sandwich."

"All the knives are dirty," she said, nodding at the dishwasher. "And there's no bread. Just come back to bed."

He knew she was doing it for spite. Twenty years ago, Soledad had begged him to stop hunting.

"It's pointless and cruel," she said, "when there's plenty in supermarkets."

Then last month, his friend Ronnie had brought over a few venison steaks and roasts, extra from his hunt. The piece in the fridge was all that remained.

"No," Homer said. "I can—" escaped his lips.

"And you'll *not* just pop over to the store to get bread. The store's closed. Everything's closed. People are tired. Nearly everyone this side of the Earth is in bed."

Soledad had a way of getting mad that wasn't anger; it was more like incredulity mixed with a pinch of condescension. She stood, not indignant, not with arms folded or hands on hips, but with arms loose at her sides as if to say she'd somehow given up on him, and just when he thought she'd forever given up, she smiled at one side of her mouth.

"You're exasperating, Homer," she said, breathy, woozy. "Like a little boy."

How could he argue? At this late hour, he didn't feel his age, only a sense of mischief, and that the venison was important. And he wanted to ask if she remembered prickly pear bushes in Corpus, or horny toads, the scent of bluebonnets, but he couldn't make the pieces of what he wanted to say into an argument for staying up later. Soledad closed the fridge door and marched him back to bed, a POW, sullen, though intrigued when Soledad, rolling onto her side of the mattress, took down the concrete pillow barrier between them and nuzzled his side.

* * *

"KNIVES ARE CLEAN," Soledad declared and popped the lever of the dishwasher. "At my lunch break, I'll run out and bring some bread home. Meanwhile, there's milk—and cereal."

She stood in dishwasher steam mushrooming upward, dampening, darkening the line where her graying hair met her scalp, making it look like a wig. When she removed her glasses and held them behind her to clear, he noted the two purplish spots each side of the bridge of her nose. Homer hated her minimum-wage job at the Zoo concession selling exotic stuffed animals.

"You look tired," he said.

When the steam let up, he could see the blue magnanimity in Soledad's eyes when she repeated, "I'll bring you bread," and then a gray hardness, "on my break."

"I don't need your damned bread or knives," he said. "Just be careful driving. We don't have medical insurance...I mean, for the time being."

"I'm late," she said, snapped her purse shut, rattled the car keys, and went out the door. He wanted her to slam it, to start something, anything, wanted the sound to mark the beginning of some saga between them, something starting out tragic, dark, portentous, only to be transcended at the brink of intolerable loneliness by the improbable will of each, alone, wanting and needing one another, simply, beautifully, and unapologetically, because each *was* alone.

But the door clicked softly shut behind Soledad.

Homer stood alone in the kitchen wondering exactly what he'd mean by *I don't need* because he did need: needed to get out and apply for another job that week to keep his six months of unemployment pay going. And he'd had a nibble. The Phone Zone, Akron, which meant a long commute, but it was something, a possibility since they'd called him for an interview. The office was in a strip mall, one of those 1970s deals, with glassy fronts and old aluminum window casings coated with white powdery oxidation that reminded him of flour dusting his mother's hands as she worked the yeast bread she'd made daily.

He shook his mother's bread from his thoughts, sank back into his car seat, and went over his qualifications. His standard spiel. He was an experienced mobile/iPad tester;

he'd tested numerous applications—should he say "numerous" or "many"? He'd written automated testing scripts, created test plans, test cases, defect reports, test summaries, and scads. He could work in a fast-paced environment. What else? After eighty-nine job applications and twelve interviews, it seemed he always missed one thing, some smidgen of information that might have gotten him the job, might have hit the target, like checking windage before a long shot with the Springfield. After one such miss, he recalled how Conrad removed his crumpled Houston Astros ball cap and scratched his balding head.

"Windage is left to right; why in hell'd you go messing with the elevation?"

Then Homer remembered that one thing. He was able to work with staff at multiple levels of the organization. That sounded good. Real good. But then he worried that his contacts felt dry. He'd not worn them in five or six years. His vision was different now, but he'd worn them anyway because it made him look younger, not as nerdy. But maybe they wanted nerdy? Too late, anyway. He'd left his specks at home. He removed the contacts, re-lubed his eyeballs, tapped the contacts in place, and waited a few minutes for the redness in his eyes to lessen.

When he entered the Phone Zone, he felt suitably serious and confident. He adjusted his walk like Soledad had shown him, working at not dragging his left foot, and lessening the clicking in his left knee. Long ago, he'd torn the meniscus in the knee climbing a pecan tree after a bobcat, according to Conrad another "lame-brained predicament" he'd gotten himself into. He fell out of the tree, caught his knee in the crook of two limbs, hanging from it like a frightened monkey until Conrad got him down with a stepladder.

Homer approached the store manager.

"Hi, I'm Homer Lynch," he said, then felt another hiccup-laugh in his chest when he spied the man's nameplate, "Mr. Wamboldt." He was a young man, with burly hair like you might find on a man's chest—but on his head; he had thick glasses with dark horn rims that made Homer rub his own irritated eyes in regret he'd not worn his nerdy specks.

"Yes. Lynch," the young man said. "Alright, then."

He reached across the desk, took Homer's hand, then Wamboldt's derrière began to descend into his seat, all the while hanging onto Homer's hand, such that Homer could feel himself tipping dangerously toward the front edge of Wamboldt's desk. When the young man let go, Homer felt himself snap backwards into his own seat, knee clicking, chair casters screeching a little against the old clay tiles.

"I'm glad to meet you," Homer said.

"Are you good with computers, Mr. Lynch?" Wamboldt asked without looking up from Homer's application sheet.

"Of course, I'm good with computers," Homer replied. "I worked a long time as a software tester for Global Vibes."

"I'm afraid I couldn't find you on LinkedIn."

"What's LinkedIn?"

Wamboldt looked up, startled, and set Homer's application aside.

Homer began his spiel while the young man nodded and grunted, then Wamboldt ceremoniously slipped a hand in his pocket under his desk, which gave Homer cause to pause briefly, thinking the young man was about to play with himself, then sighed when he heard the tinkle of coins in the man's pocket, but wondered if it really amounted to the same thing as masturbating.

"Mobile/iPad," Homer said, "many applications," he went on, "fast-paced environment," he smiled, thinking that had to do the trick. Then, his *coup de grâce*, "multiple levels of the organization…"

"Impressive," Wamboldt said. "Maybe you can tell me what would make you a good fit for Phone Zone in particular. We're really looking for an entry-level salesperson with some technical background. But someone with pizzazz."

There it was again, Homer thought, the overqualified card, played to avoid revealing the other card he held back in his hand—the overage card.

He thought fast.

"Well," he said and produced a smile that reeked of pizzazz, "a cell phone's like a Springfield rifle sight. There are times when you need to adjust the windage, times when you need to fiddle with the elevation, and sometimes both. It's a delicate thing. I think I can help your customers target the phone that's right for them."

Brilliant, Homer thought. He'd bagged the job for sure. He imagined if Conrad were there, how he'd be beaming with pride at Homer's homegrown wisdom. But when he heard the coins in Wamboldt's pocket stop clinking, he knew otherwise.

"Thanks for coming all this way, Mr. Lynch," Wamboldt said. "We'll call you if we can find a place for you at the Phone Zone."

* * *

WHEN HOMER RETURNED home, the house was cold, Cleveland cold, which meant wet cold. The thermostat clicked. Fire rumbled in the burners. He went into the hallway and set the thermostat lower. The house got colder, creaked. He put on a sweater jacket, crumpled some paper, tossed it in the fireplace, then set a handful of kindling on top. He headed for the basement, pausing a moment at the bottom step to marvel that he hadn't yet forgotten why he'd come down. He found an armload of two-by-four scrap pieces he'd saved from various projects and went back upstairs. He set the scrap pieces on the kindling, then set the little heap on fire. After a time, the pine tar in the scrap wood sizzled and popped. A couple times, he had to quickly pluck steaming charcoal bits from the carpet and fling them back onto the grate. But the radiant heat on his face satisfied him in a way he'd not been in a long time, a heat he'd made, not the Suburban Gas Company, and as time went on, he began to feel what he'd meant by *I don't need*, the way he'd felt long ago hunting swamp rabbit with Conrad's .22, cutting sticky flesh from fur, roasting it on open flames until the rabbit spit grease, as if in retaliation for his having killed it—not needing was nothing more than that, no more than a piece of venison in a fridge, a cold house, and a little heat, a sense that he could overcome both without running to the store, which actually meant driving to the store in the Fiesta, their second car, sure to be sold to pay the mortgage, which meant burning gasoline, stuff priced like gold. *I don't need*, he thought, and that seemed to satisfy most everything, all but his hunger. He sat by the fire of his making until the last orange ember flashed black, reasoning he might stay by the fire a little longer if he could stand perfectly still such that the cold air molecules would not bump him and absorb his body heat.

Later, he went into the bathroom, stoppered and ran tepid water in the tub. He stripped and soaked himself there, trying to rid himself of all things Wamboldt, dreading the moment he'd need to come out and face the ruthless air molecules again. When he did, he left the tub stoppered, toweled off, dressed quickly, then filled the bathroom sink with hot water, and shaved, leaving flecks of whiskers and clouds of lather to float there, thinking the heat from both sink and bathwater would transfer to the house and not be wasted down the drain.

He went back into the kitchen, found his mother's old mixing bowl, a small sack of sugar, another of flour, oil, and a packet of dry yeast. He mixed all in the bowl with warm water. He beat the dough down, beat it a long time, until his knuckles felt red and clean, and then he beat it more, remembering Conrad hollering.

"When I said get that gator, I didn't mean go *into* the swamp for it!"

Homer was hip-high in the water, watching two nubs of the gator's eyes unzip the surface. They zigged then zagged directly for him. He slid the Springfield's ancient bolt back, heard the round click into the breech, nudged the bolt forward, locked it, and shot the mustard-eyed monster of the marsh. It rolled fast, thrashing in water, fast and hard and viciously, as if every ounce of the monster's life force were contained in those final sounds of its beating water—then it was suddenly calm, water gently breaking at the exposed roots of bald cypresses. While he and Conrad hauled the dead eight-foot, snaggle-toothed monster back to their pickup, he figured the gator'd bring at least fifty bucks. Conrad should have been happy about that, but he didn't speak until they were halfway back to Corpus.

"You're a fuckin' idiot. You know that, Homer?"

I don't need, he thought, then nearly laughed, a spasm that came out more like a hiccup. He didn't need to know why he felt so proud of being Conrad's fuckin' idiot. He just was.

Homer found an old dishrag, wet it with warm water from the faucet, draped it over the dough in his mother's mixing bowl, and set it in a square of sunlight slanting in the kitchen window from the backyard. Then he went into a closet, found a stack of jigsaw puzzles Soledad'd bought him to pass the time: countless thousands, no, tens of thousands of puzzle pieces, the whole of which were supposed to represent places like Uruguay, Kansas, and a covered bridge in Maine, or was it Vermont? He opened a box, spilled Venice onto the kitchen table, groped, then picked through its pieces, interconnected them, guided by only the subtlest differences in shape and coloring, guessing how they may fit into the overall picture, how the rippled water of the canal reflected some other version of the orange-pink-green buildings, broken by the undulating folds into vibrant, unstructured colors.

When Soledad came home from work on her lunch break, she went straight into the bathroom. He heard her pull the stoppers from the tub and sink, water gurgling in the drains. When she arrived in the kitchen, she carried a loaf of bread by its neck, like a small game kill. She swung the bread onto the counter near the cupboards, then discovered Homer sitting at the table with the completed puzzle of Venice.

"What's up with the water in the sink and tub?" she asked. "Did you make a fire on that old grate?"

He wanted to explain his personal theories of heat conservation, but his mind clouded in anticipation of her asking about his job interview. She didn't, had obviously forgotten. His thoughts seemed to swirl and gurgle in a drain, lost.

"Yeah," he said, answering her second question, first, then rotated Venice a little to draw her attention to it.

"For a Texas boy, only once transplanted to Cleveland," she laughed and kissed him square on the top of his bald head, "you're getting to be well-traveled."

"I suppose," he mumbled.

But the traveling was over. Soledad was home. She crossed the kitchen to the window, then lifted and peeked under the dishrag covering the mixing bowl.

"Homer, I told you I'd be bringing bread home," she said, arms hanging at her side, helpless, incriminating. Then she softened, and said, "You're impossible."

* * *

AFTER SOLEDAD WENT back to work, he realized: He wasn't impossible. He was possible. He was a thousand miles possible, the distance he'd come north from Texas with Soledad for a job that now deserted him, one that now left him a cold, unemployed puzzle master in a strange land. But if being stranded and jobless in Cleveland was what being possible meant, he wanted no part of it. He was sick of being that kind of possible. Mobile possible. He supposed it all began when he refused to make the venison sandwich from Soledad's store-bought bread. It would be impossible for him to design, construct, and operate a bread factory, but it was possible to dredge deep from memory Eva making yeast bread, vivid as on the mornings when he stood eye-high at her counter, watching her knead with tiny, powerful, flour-dusted hands. It was possible for him to make, to taste, to take sustenance from Eva's glorious bread after all these years. Handmade. Homemade. Made. Felt. Possible. He remembered Eva's excitement, finding him in some far corner of the house, seizing him by the elbow and marching him into the kitchen, lifting the damp dishrag from her mixing bowl, the intoxicating scent of yeast.

"Look, son," he remembered her saying. "It has risen!"

And after a time, so did Homer's bread, his beautiful, possible, holy bread.

He preheated the oven, floured a bread pan, transferred the dough to it, and slid it onto the rack.

While the bread baked, he went into the basement. In a bottom drawer of his workbench, he found the old hot pot he'd used long ago to melt lead in for casting .30-06 bullets for the Springfield. It was still half-full of old lead. He set his old kerosene camp stove on the workbench, opened a window high near the rafters to vent, set the hot pot on the stove, and lit it with a pop. While the lead melted, he found a short section of copper pipe that had been capped, leftover from the plumber installing their new water heater. By the time he located his old spoon for skimming slag, the lead had melted, the slag black and spitting on top. He removed the slag, then clamped the copper pipe in his vice. He found a narrow, flat piece of scrap iron, and inserted it into the pipe. He held the pipe in one hand with an oven mitt, and with the other poured the molten lead into the pipe. After the lead cooled and solidified around the scrap iron, he removed his creation from the vise, filled a Maxwell House can with water, then doused it. Spitting and hissing, a crude creature emerged from the water, quickly made, shabby—but possible. He sharpened his creation with a flat file, then whetstone, and took the homemade knife upstairs, opened the smooching fridge and, at long last, seized the patient piece of venison, and sliced from it a gloriously thick hunk.

He removed the bread from the oven, leaving the door down to recover heat into the house. While the oven cooled, ticking, he carefully sliced two pieces of yeast bread with his creation, set one on a plate, centered a piece of venison, and covered it gingerly with the second slice. He arranged the plate with the sandwich, knife alongside, the loaf of bread nearby, and just looked at it, how beautiful it was, how possible, because he had made all of it with memories and things close at hand. Then he sliced the sandwich in half, a perfect diagonal cut, the final stroke.

He ate the cold venison sandwich.

He smiled.

He teared-up and removed his contacts.

Then he made another sandwich and sliced it, not like the first, but cut parallel to the sides of the bread, and neatly arranged the sandwich, loaf, and his new knife for Soledad to find when she returned home from work. He went back to the basement to clean up. When he set the hot pot back into its drawer and tried to shove the drawer closed, it stopped short. It was then he found his old Springfield, hidden twenty years behind his workbench, wrapped in one of Conrad's old sleeveless tees spotted with Hoppe's 9 and gun blue. Twenty years and there it was, twenty after Soledad had made him dispose of the ammunition at the police station, and he had, but also twenty that he'd hidden the Springfield itself from her.

"I don't want that thing in my house!" she declared, and added, "I swear I'm leaving if you don't get rid of it."

He knew, he knew, but he couldn't bear let it go. Now, the stock was dry, faded, and cracked in places, the barrel spotted with rust. He took Conrad's tee, a can of linseed oil, and rubbed the stock a good while until the color was uniform and the wood smooth. He soaked a Q-tip with gun blue and dotted the barrel with it, then wiped the barrel with the tee. He rewrapped the Springfield in Conrad's old shirt and set it back behind the workbench.

* * *

HE HEARD SOLEDAD come in and he headed upstairs. When he reached the kitchen, she was pulling off her coat, one arm in, one out, hovering over his arrangement of the homemade knife, yeast bread, and the *pièce de résistance*, the delicately cut venison sandwich. Her coat slipped from the remaining arm, and she tossed it onto the back of a chair. She turned to look at him.

"I forgot to ask," she said, "how'd your interview go?"

"The sandwich is for you," he said.

"Homer, how did it go?"

He nodded at the sandwich.

"I made it from scratch," he said. "It's for you."

Soledad dropped into the chair before the sandwich like a lead shot.

"What do we need this bread for?" she said. "And this crude knife? Jesus, you made it from lead? Isn't that poisonous? How's anyone supposed to use it?"

Homer tried to make a sentence for her that contained everything, his theory of being possible, of needing less, of standing so still cold air molecules could not touch you and drain your heat, of stoppering sinks and tubs, of Conrad and Eva. Being possible. Being mindful. Being less. Just being.

"Soledad—" he said.

"What's the matter with you!" she shouted.

Everything he'd piled high in his mind, so high he could not sense the top, came tumbling down. He turned, went down to the basement, and got the Springfield. He let Conrad's t-shirt slip to the floor, then put on a jacket, went out the front door, and sat on the concrete slab with the rifle across his knees.

The middle school nearby had let out. A boy was skateboarding in the cul-de-sac, nearly impossible with patches of ice crusted on the street. Still, the boy dragged the board over the obstacles to small patches of bare cement, then rolled along until he crashed into another and nearly went flying, headlong. A girl was in the cul-de-sac, too, walking, mittened hand pressing a cell phone to the side of her face. Homer hiccupped. He knew all about cell phones, but he'd be damned if he could make one, and this had always bothered him, until a little later when he saw the boy and girl collide, the phone skitter across the ice then scrape over the pavement, the skateboard fly vertically, then nosedive into the concrete. The girl and boy lay side-by-side on the pavement a few moments, perfectly still, long enough that Homer started to lift the Springfield off his knees to go and see if he could help them, when, without acknowledging one another, each stuck an elbow to the pavement, jacked themselves standing, and went separate ways.

Homer wondered: Had they been less, lying there, side by side, no skateboard, no cell, just lying there, near one another? Had they?

He sat on the porch a long time, waiting for the winter sun to lose itself in the west, until the cul-de-sac was empty. It was cold, but his knees seemed warm where the Springfield rested. He heard the storm door open and shut behind him, then sensed Soledad over him.

Her voice trembled.

"Homer, what are you going to do with that?"

"This?" he asked in his little boy voice, but he knew she meant the Springfield. He lifted the butt a little and ran a hand over the stock. "I don't know."

When Soledad went back inside, he waited to hear her sobbing, or on the telephone with someone, perhaps the police. Sometimes, he got afraid like that, not afraid for himself, but afraid he'd made her afraid, though he meant no harm. But she was quiet. The house was quiet. The street was quiet. All over, things were dreadfully quiet, and there was little else to be had as the winter night came on, just the faint smell of gun blue and new stain on the old stock of the Springfield. A single memory, a pinprick in the skin of time. Conrad had been right. Just eighty-two days without work, and he'd already made an end of things.

THE PONCE DE LEÓN
SENIOR THERAPY SWIM

MOODY LIMPS FROM parking lot to main entrance. Before he can recall taking his daily doses of new statins, of Cholester-Awl and Osteo-Buttress, swish go the doors, a little wet smooch trailing. He stops, waits, looks about, thinks the doors stand agape for someone else, then realizes they stand gaping for him, just him, only him, and he inches ahead, enveloped in dank primeval warmth, a swirling atmospheric soup, like the dawn of time. He gags on chlorine, feels swept along in a swill of procreative chemicals, like the first single-cell organism in Creation, jiggling cilia to move forward, close along one wall, into the steamy senior men's locker room, until he confronts a tract of olive-drab slime growing in the grout of a tile. Moody recoils, fearing he may contract MRSA on top of the torn meniscus in his left knee, the result of a sixteen-year old's jumping low-line sidekick in the martial arts class Moody enrolled in at age sixty, the injury Moody's fault, part of the dojo creed: You get hurt, it's your fault. Everything is your fault, all the time.

Another spasm of pain ripples from his knee to groin, so Moody ventures farther into the locker room, until the fog begins to part, slowly, peeling away eons of anticipation in seconds—and at last, he encounters three monstrous figures in dim drizzle, old men sitting on benches, buck naked, sagging, puckered ass cracks galore, all in various stages of dragging on swim trunks in terrifying slow motion. One has an eight-inch incision running vertically along his spine, scars of suture blooming like tiny violets on either side of the wound. The man rises, snugs his trunks with a sound like a last gasp, and shish-shushes baby steps toward the exit to the pool. Then a second senior brushes slowly past Moody, examining him on his way out with one raised bushy eyebrow sprouting a stiff wild hair above the others. The third man has thoroughly tangled his street pants and swim trunks about his ankles. He rises and faces Moody, swings his old, wrinkled, pendulous dong square in Moody's view, and pleads with his eyes, no effort of human speech, just pleads silently, as if Moody is his Paleolithic manservant. Moody goes over and tries to untangle the man's pants and trunks—too-big, floppy, printed with little pimply Howdy Doody faces. He realizes he can't unknot the man's tangled trunks unless he kneels, the old man's dong hanging just at his forehead.

After Moody leaves old Tangled Pants diddling with his trunks' tie-string, he changes in a modestly secluded area of the locker room, then exits through another set of wet smooching doors—and there it is, the Ponce de León, what passes for a Fountain of Youth, gold paint trimming the perimeter of the rectangular pool, chest-high water, a vague plume of antediluvian mist rising from the surface, a rousing scent of fecundity—if not for the gray heads lumbering at random through the sloshing, virescent liquid, looking like survivors of a shipwreck. A teenage girl, the lifeguard, perches above all, like an angel divining who will be saved from the marine calamity and who will not.

Above the chlorine smog is an enormous mural of Juan Ponce de León, painted onto garish green cinderblocks. He wears a mustard-yellow doublet high about his neck, a half-armor breast plate, and is topped with an ornate morion with red-white-red plumes. Diagonally dividing Juan is a green sash terminating in a rapier and its blue scabbard. Juan points with one finger, left. At first, Moody thinks he must be pointing off-mural, at something like the mythical Fountain of Youth, though his eyes, gazing in the same direction as his fingertips, are open too wide to be regal, and not wide enough to be stunned by some amazing New World discovery. Rather, he seems to be looking at Moody, like he's one of his old Conquistador pals, as if to say, "Don't I know you? Where've you been all these years?" Juan seems to tell Moody to dive right in, to say the legendary restorative waters are fine; only Moody wonders, if the water is so wonderful, then why are so many old fish sloshing about, barely keeping their gasping geriatric gills going? Statistically, there ought to be one or two individuals in some stage of youthful retrogression in Juan's Golden Pond.

So accosted by the eyes of Juan Ponce de León, Moody blurs his come-hither orbs and examines the background of the mural: some unknown, verdant cove, on which bobs a small three-masted galleon, inscribed *Santa María de la Consolación*. But he doesn't need consolation, doesn't want to cast off into the uncertain seas of the Senior Therapy Swim. He doesn't need anyone. Maybe he can live with the pain? He turns to flee the formidable Fountain, then runs smack-chest into Tangled Pants, so close he can smell the morning oatmeal on his breath.

Tangled Pants ceremoniously pops an orange pill in his mouth. He swallows twice.

"Water pill," he says.

Moody wonders why Tangled Pants tells him this, recalls that "water pill" is what his father used to call it, and it kept his father up nights whizzing in the bathroom. Then, suddenly, the diuretic cloud lifts and Moody understands—Tangled Pants is *daring* him to enter the pool with the knowledge that, in all likelihood, Tangled Pants will *pee* in the Ponce de León. Tangled Pants continues to stand there, with a kind of "join-us-if-you-dare" stare. Moody feels his flight instinct kick in again, but how can he go without explaining before he shoves

Tangled Pants aside and tears off? How can he, with the man's dare lingering in the halogen haze?

He tells Tangled Pants, "I'm just here for my knee. That's all."

He rubs his kneecap in an exaggerative way in case the old man's hard of hearing.

But Tangled Pants continues to block his way with the same join-the-club whimsy on his face. Moody wishes just once he could say one small thing about his bad knee to another person without opening Pandora's Medicine Chest, without their words flying out to torment the world.

Words like, *Tell me about it!*

Or, *It's downhill from here on.*

And his favorite, *Be glad that's all that's wrong with you!*

He waits for Tangled Pants to unleash his scrap of medical mayhem, and he does.

"Getting old is mandatory," flies out Tangled Pants's mouth.

"Maybe," Moody mumbles.

But Tangled Pants still isn't budging, and by now Moody's meniscus is killing him—he's going to show Tangled Pants what old is *not*. He swings around with all the youthful vigor he can muster, limp-skips to the Dutch Masters cigar box, drops in a dollar bill, and heads for the pile of swim accessories his doctor wanted him to try, which means a mountain of multi-colored foam floating noodles, canoodling with one another at random, the way a tangled wad of fossilized worms looks in an archeological concretion.

He grabs a fluorescent orange noodle, tugs it from the massive wad, then slowly steps into the hottish water, all the while scouting for a shipping lane clear enough to see him safely through the primal sea of seniors. After a time, he finds one, pushes the noodle in front of him, folded in a vee like a cow catcher, and starts marching in his lane, high-stepping, far higher than the doctor had ordered. He wants to be different than the ghost-grays drifting about him. Soon, Wild Hair passes Moody, and behind him glides Violet Spine, then a newcomer comes into view, a pale woman, someone Moody guesses must be of enormous submerged proportions judging by the size of the wake she pushes at her sides, what surfers call snappers, swells that just begin to curl. Her eyes are pinpoints surrounded by a sea of wrinkled flesh, a veritable Mabel Dick chugging through an ocean of gray heads. He goosesteps right, allows extra distance between himself and Mabel in case he's hit by the undetermined tonnage beneath the surface.

After the close encounter with Mabel Dick, he hangs on his noodle by his armpits, bicycles his legs underwater, in place, reasoning that he's less likely to stray into a crowd.

From time to time, he absent-mindedly kicks with his left leg, feels a jolt of pain in his meniscus, a reminder that, because it's a ligament, it will never heal completely. Mabel Dick passes by on her second go-around. Her wash sloshes in Moody's mouth, water he assumes diluted with who knows how many volumes of senior pee. He spits a couple times, then gets out of the water, leaves his orange noodle poolside for later, then goes to get his stretchy thing from his locker.

Most all the seniors have noodles, but Moody's the only one with his stretchy thing in the pool. He shows his rubber rope with a bit of flourish, untangling it from one stirrup and swinging it like an expensive pocket watch on a gold chain, then stands on the bottom step leading into the water, hooks one stirrup onto his left foot, and ties the other end to the steel safety railing. He enters the water, stretches the rope taut so his left knee gets tension, then works his bad leg slowly back and forth through the water.

Soon, Tangled Pants glides his way, closer, closer, so close he gets all wrapped up in Moody's Stretchy Thing, so much so that the remaining tension in the rope drags Moody's left leg toward the steel railing. Moody's good leg slips beneath him, and he descends backwards into the water, getting a mouthful of the awful piss-laced liquid. He butts Tangled Pants with his bad knee and pain rockets up Moody's leg. Tangled groans, turns his tired chin and pleading eyes to the lifeguard, who leaps nimbly to the edge of the Ponce de León.

She says, in the weirdest kind of pubescent, matronly tone, "Sir, you'll have to take the rope out of the pool."

Moody's okay with that; he doesn't belong in the pool, anyway. Why should he expect any other treatment? But then it happens, one thing that breaks the noodle's back. Tangled Pants gets out of the water, onto the deck, and swipes Moody's orange noodle. He seems very smug about it, too. Tangled shuffles down the steps, back into the pool, with both his white noodle and Moody's orange one tucked under his armpits, peddling fast away from Moody.

Moody plots his revenge, waits until Tangled Pants finds what he must feel is a safe harbor near Wild Hair and Violet Spine. Mabel Dick waddles out of the pool using the steps near both. He's glad because his plan needs the surface of the Ponce de León to be relatively calm. He glides closer to Tangled Pants, navigates so he's a good fifteen feet behind him, then, like a stealthy Plesiosaur, submerges, mindful to close his mouth tight. Underwater, he kicks hard with his right leg, pulls with his arms, sees Tangled coming into murky view, his blurry Howdy Doody printed trunks. Moody's thinking he'll give him a howdy-doody he won't forget. He extends his arms, reaches for Tangled's trunks, ready to yank them down. He figures with one more kick, he'll make it. He kicks with all his might and realizes, too late, that he's kicked with his bad leg, which spasms, muscles going into protect-the-joint mode, all of which causes his leg to cramp. He surfaces with a whoosh of air from his lungs, thrashes water with his arms, yelps something like, "Shit-uh!" and goes under again. Next thing he knows, there's an enormous concussion that thunders through the water, like a depth charge going off, and he feels a powerful arm about his chest and chin, his head out, taking in air and water, coughing his guts out until he's dragged from the water and set down on the deck, lying on his back.

Overhead, Juan Ponce de León presides. At this angle, his eyes seem to gaze through the watery haze heavenward, poised to wag his conquering finger over Moody in the sign of the Cross; last rites.

Someone says, "For a minute there, we thought you were about to leave us."

Then they're all hovering above him. Wild Hair, Violet Spine, Tangled Pants, the lifeguard, and Moody's savior, Mabel Dick, who cannonballed into the Ponce de León to rescue him.

"There, there, just lie still," Mabel Dick says.

She pats his hand.

And he ought to be grateful—he guesses he is—but can't help thinking he's heard words like theirs before: "you were about to leave us," and "just lie still," and then it flat-out hits him, how long, long ago he went to see the

Wizard of Oz, and at the very end they're all hovering over Dorothy's bed, Wild Hair like the Lion, Violet Spine the Tin Man, Tangled Pants the Scarecrow, and Mabel Dick her Aunt Em, all their kind, wise old faces looking down at him—Dorothy—who has so much her elders can give her, Dorothy, their initiate, Dorothy, getting older, on the cusp of becoming what they are, only it's the opposite—instead of learning things from them, like Dorothy, Wild Hair takes away his courage, Violet Spine his heart, Tangled Pants his brain, and Aunt Em all his remaining human sympathy.

He doesn't know where Uncle Henry, the Professor, and Toto are, and doesn't care.

Moody feebly flails once at Tangled Pants's swim trunks, wants to drag them down, but the lifeguard slaps his arm away. He reaches right, finds the orange noodle Tangled Pants has dropped, hugs it to his side. Someone—he thinks the lifeguard—keeps asking if he wants her to call 911, but he's thinking you don't have 911 in dreams, and this can be no more than a dream.

"I don't need 911!" he says, "I need—"

But doesn't know what he needs.

He grabs his left leg, wincing with pain.

They all want to help. After a short struggle, someone tugs his noodle from his arms and puts it under his head. Another's got his pulse. One goes for a capsule of the new super pain killer, Elysium.

"Heaven!" Moody howls when someone jams the capsule in his mouth, followed by—horrors! —more water, in a Dixie cup.

They all gather around him, draw closer, in a strange kind of twilight.

"You can't help me," he tells them. "It's my fault. All my fault. Really, don't do that. Don't fuss. Stop touching me! I can't stay here. I'm not one of you. I just want to go home. There's no place like home. Please, let me go home."

But there's a luminous liquid night behind their ancient round faces, a feeling he's not at the dawn of anything, not a dark warm sea where chemicals swarm in accidental creation, but some awful, medicinal, intended end, a place where all is well, all forgotten, all healed.

LA LENGUA SERPENTINA

Educate yourself to silence.
                                     —Daumier, Fellini's *8 ½*

WHEN, SUDDENLY, ANTONIA discovered, as one only discovers when her dreams are remembered in a waking stupor, that she no longer dreamed in lovely forms—of the urn; the saucer; the upturned shallow bowl, like a breast; the deep, pendulous shape of the penis—but only sounds—gibberish, the racket of remembered events—she went and found her mother, who was cooking lentils, an older woman, for Antonia was nearly forty herself.

"Mama," she said, "I no longer see things in my dreams."

"You are lucky, child," she replied, for Antonia's mother still called her child. "You are lucky you still dream at all. Count your blessings. I've stopped dreaming."

So Antonia made a dish of couscous, pale yellow, and sprinkled it with bits of green and red peppers, mint, and carrot. She dabbed her spoon in the colorful, fragrant heap of couscous, but did not eat; at last, she put a spoonful of tahini on top, then pushed the dish from her and went to her room at the top of the stairs. There, in the middle of the day, she dozed as she often did, feeling a pang of sadness for her mother. She closed her eyes and heard the slapping of the little pellets in the hem of the curtain against the windowsill, and under her eyelids made colors and shapes from the light trapped in her eyes: blue and purple and green clouds. Then, with the weak light in the room coming through the thicket of veins in her eyelids, she made red clouds of all shapes—and these, all these clouds of all shapes, became the nearest substitute for the shapes and colors she remembered had been in her dreams as a younger woman.

But when she, at last, dropped off, her sleep was dark and dreamless, and through the terrible exactness of perfect darkness, she heard only the sound of her brother's laughter in the backyard, her brother who long ago had moved away from home to college, then from college to Vietnam, and died there in the war. Then, in her dream made of only sounds, she remembered thinking that her window was open and that the curtain was slapping the sill, that she might be hearing him laughing in reality through the open window. Then, she recalled he was dead, even as she slept she remembered this, and when she awoke remembered only two things: that she had heard him laughing and that he was dead. And there was one thing more, not a memory, but a feeling about the sound of his laughter, something distinct that stayed with her. She could not take the sound from the place inside her and make it with her mouth, and she could not make the sound by thinking it in her brain, and she could not use the feeling of the sound to bring her brother's face back to her; she could not know the time and place the sound had occurred because the sound had no time or place, nothing, and it wouldn't come into her mind or mouth or eyes.

* * *

IN THE MORNING, Antonia watched her mother's hand tremble in the light coming from the window over the kitchen sink. She wanted to tell her mother about the sound in her dream, but she hadn't the words to describe it. So she left her mother standing at the window, a cigarette in one hand, its glowing tip quivering in the light.

At the bakery where she worked, a block from her mother's house in Montauk, Antonia worked dough with her hands, feeling its cool, floured surface in her palms. She slapped the dough on the table, pausing a moment as a tiny refrain from the radio on the shelf above her died out. She switched the radio off and continued to work the dough with her hands, listening for the thump of the dough on the table and feeling the thump in her hands. She tried to hold the sound of the dough on the table in her hands as long as she could, but knew they would be calling for the dough soon; they would bake it and sell it; she knew that no matter how many times she tried to make the improbable nexus of feeling and sound in her hands, she would need to give it away.

After work, she took her bicycle and rode it to a small city park, Kirk Park, near Montauk Pond. She rode along a narrow grassy path with wild roses leaning in at all sides. The path led to a small dock connected to a covered pavilion. She set the bicycle on the grayed floor beams of the pavilion and saw two empty wine glasses and a bottle of red wine, half-full, sitting in the center of the floor. She looked all around but saw no one, and she shuddered a moment, feeling isolated, seeing only the little waves rolling over the pond with the wind, over themselves, making translucent shadows in their shallow crests and valleys. She looked for other people across the pond, on other docks and jetties poking into the water; yet, remarkably, she was entirely alone.

She stood in the pavilion for a long time, looking at the wine glasses and the half-empty bottle of wine. Then, she knelt on the planks near them and tipped one glass on its side, and in her perfect solitude, while looking at the two curvaceous shapes, their stems, and the bottle near them, placed just so, a sound came from her dream, a bit of sound broken out from all the others she'd heard in her brother's laughter.

"*Ka*," she whispered.

When she first made the sound, it seemed hollow, simple, empty, and in no way referred to the bottle and glasses she saw on the floor of the pavilion. She thought of making the sound again but looked about and saw two young women standing on the pier across the pond. She shuddered at the idea of others hearing it. She feared she might let the sound slip from her lips later at work or react to a string of similar sounds made by another person. As hollow and small as it was, the sound seemed precious to her. So she let the idea of repeating the sound slip away, left the bottle and glasses on the floor of the pavilion, and bicycled home, keeping the bit of sound all to herself.

* * *

ANTONIA NUDGED THE edge of a small slip of white paper, upon which her mother had written that she would be spending the night with a friend in the City, the West Village. Antonia poked at the little note until it moved into the center of the kitchen table, then she rotated it with a finger so the corners did not quite align themselves with the corners of the table. Seeing the note in this attitude, she suddenly wanted to say something to her mother. Her wants often exceeded her knowledge of what was possible. She even wanted her mother's friend in the Village to be possible, a sculptor she didn't particularly like, an impossible man with black paint under his nails and tiny white spots of paint all over his hands. She didn't like him because he was too quiet and spoke in whispers, and only about his work, which seemed strange and disconnected to her: here a bicycle handle, a surfboard, a piece of petrified dung; the rest of the time, he was inside himself. But for her mother's sake, she wanted the impossible man to be possible, even though she was sure he would never care to listen to her mother's indecipherable sorrow. Antonia wanted only what she knew was not possible.

So, seeing her mother's note, the bit of white paper, just out of kilter with the larger, flat white surface of the Formica table, and thinking about the impossible man, another fragment from the laughter she remembered her dead brother make in her dream came to her.

"*La.*"

And she was silent, inside herself the rest of the evening, not saying anything, keeping her new sound close to her in perfect silence. She did not speak, even under her breath, even for the sake of herself or the wallpaper or the sofa, and after a time of this silence, she began to know that she was entirely inside herself and knew that she spited the wallpaper and the sofa with her silence, and she enjoyed this, enjoyed keeping everything away from even the inanimate things around her. Then, she thought, hiding her new sounds all the while, and forming her thoughts instead from pure feeling and nothing else, *Who can be more silent than this?*

Later, in her bedroom, in her house alone, without her mother or the impossible man from the Village, she tried to dream a dream other than one of her brother laughing in the backyard, but she couldn't. Nothing came to her and she slept like a dead woman.

The next morning, she felt numb while she worked at the bakery, kneading, rolling, and cutting the dough into doughnuts. She closed her eyes each time she cut the doughnut shapes out. She had cut the shapes before this way, hundreds of times, but now couldn't bear the act of cutting into the dough, something she'd felt so intimately with her hands.

After work, she again bicycled to the little city park and dock and pavilion. As she walked out along the dock, she noticed that the wine glasses and bottle were gone, and in their place sat three mallard ducks, two with the bright green and red markings of a male, and a small, brownish duck, a female. Antonia paused and wondered if she might approach them without scaring them away; then, seeing that they were unaware of her, she watched them from the dock, recalling again the sound of her brother's laughter in the dream she could only feel, and another bit of sound suddenly broke out from the memory of the feeling of her brother's laughter in her dream.

"*Roo*," she whispered at the ducks.

* * *

THAT NIGHT, SHE came home and found her mother alone, sleeping at the table in the kitchen, her cheek resting on the hard surface. An empty wine glass sat near the note her mother had written to her the day before. The glass had a pinkish ring in the bottom where the wine had evaporated and a bit of lipstick smudged just below the lip. Antonia pushed a finger gently at the base of the wine glass, moved it near her mother's cheek, and left the kitchen. She paced the house quietly. For a short time, she believed she'd managed it—a revelry of silence beyond all that could ever hurt her again, the long, forgotten impressions of grief and loneliness, her secret sounds hers, no one's but hers. She sat awhile in a chair by the picture window with her eyes closed, with no other need but to keep the silence all there to herself…and her mother?

She went back to the kitchen, where her mother continued to sleep, and leaned close to her ear.

"*Ka,*" she whispered, but her mother did not move. "*Ka…La…Roo…*" she said softly and waited, wanting some sign of stirring, the tiniest flinch in the most delicate lines of muscle in her mother's eyelids, but none came.

Her mother did not stir. The house did not stir. Nor did the things in the house she had spited with her silence. But neither did the sadness inside her in the same perplexing way. She went to her room upstairs, where the curtains rustled against the sill, the night air against her skin. Alone, before falling asleep, she practiced the serpentine tongue again, clear and wordless, perfect and simple, a language without bounds, the purest song she knew and could sing to no one.

VIGIL FOR *AMMOSPIZA*
NIGRÉSCENS

I AM IN BED.

Dreaming, sleeping next to Bill. No, it's not a dream. It's a song.

> *Let me tell you how it used to be;*
> *let me tell you about the wind*
> *and the reign of the salty sea.*

I am singing this to myself. Funny song. How does my subconscious know there is a difference between *rain* and *reign*? God, I hope I don't wake Bill.

* * *

I'M AWAKE BEFORE the others.

But it isn't morning. It's dark. Pitch. I put on a light, read a little. I think about the day's meals, what they will be, what I've got to make them with, what I have to run out to get. Then my thoughts are silent, and for a moment, there is perfect silence, temporal quiet living in the corridors of water that assault the shore and come onto the beach outside. In my heart and mind, even in this fleeting and complete silence inside myself, during these nights I've spent at the beach house, I listen closely for two things: first, sounds outside the beach house, the rush of water coming in, columning in soft piles, running over cold laps of dark sand; second, the sounds of Bill, sounds that he may be waking, stirring in a bad dream, uneasy or hungry. I listen for the wake of each watery onslaught of unsettled ocean, that moment when each head of each wave expends its energy crawling over the beach—when waves embark on their ways back to populaces of sea things—what moment of silence, I listen for Bill in our bedroom—or the return of the surf—and I know I'll remember only one thing about that moment: perfect silence.

* * *

IT IS STILL dark, almost dawn.

I am standing on the beach near our jetty. I hear the surf, but I can't see it. There are lights out at sea, straight out, trying to illuminate the horizon, but they fail. They are not points of light, but an aggregation of points, a cruise ship, maybe a tanker. Here in Florida, big ships never come that close to shore. Bill says it's a problem with draft. In Alaska, I remember the party ships navigating the craggy coast, gliding in close: at night these ships were myriad windowpanes of light, like glowing compound eyes searching for passage. I think about my mother and father, who led the most ordinary lives.

* * *

I'M ON THE jetty now.

Can't see the pilings. I feel suspended over the water, like I have no feet. I stop at the end of the jetty. The air is warm. I imagine the continental shelf running under the sea, how it slants out, begins so shallow, travels hundreds of miles and inclines only slightly. I want to know the larger order of things. Things. I could never make it out to where the continental shelf drops-off to the bottom of the sea. The thought of walking it is wearisome. Why do I bother imagining it? It's too far to go.

* * *

THE OTHERS ARE awake.

They stand all around me, yawning. Light is everywhere. Dominique forages for coffee in the kitchen. Howie, Bill's old Army buddy, goes out on the deck overlooking the ocean. I am creaming egg yolks in the kitchen and watching Bill. He is bare-ass naked under his maroon bathrobe, in his white socks, slip-sliding on the polished wood floor; he reminds me of Charlie Chaplin in *Modern Times*; he is like an overexposed movie showing in the wide mouth of morning light coming into the room. He glides across the room, armchair to armchair, his legs like thin bell clappers, coming down, out of his robe, moving rapidly, unsurely. First, he stops at Dominique's chair, kneels, and rests his hand on her arm.

"Please, Dom," he pleads. "It'll be fun." He puts his lips together and says with his best Tweety Bird: "Pwiddee pweez, Dom?"

* * *

NOW BILL IS telling Dom about his rare Dusky Seaside Sparrow.

"*Ammospiza nigréscens*," Bill grumbles when I've forgotten its proper name.

He says scientists think they have the last bird of its kind in a cage at an institute a few miles up the coast. *A few miles*, Bill says, like it's important that his rare bird is only minutes away by car, within our grasp. But Bill doesn't believe the scientists. He is obsessed with getting Dom to go with him to look for the bird in the salt marshes. She isn't interested. Dom gets up and joins me in the kitchen.

* * *

HOWIE COMES IN, sits, and begins to go through the *Wall Street Journal*.

Bill crawls on his hands and knees over to Howie's chair, takes an edge of his newspaper down with his finger and peers in: "I'll just get the dinghy, some beer, and chips—a day's survival kit—and we'll search for the critter; what do you say, How?"

Howie ignores Bill's lobbying. He says: "The Market is coming back. I'm calling my broker." Then Howie looks past Bill, and he calls over to me: "Okay if I use your phone, Nessa? I won't be long."

"Sure," I tell him, coming in from the kitchen with the eggs. I sit at the table. I smile at Howie, despite his referring to me as Nessa, short, I suppose, for Vanessa, though I've never heard my name corrupted in quite that way. Then I'm cringing inside, remembering Bill likes to call me Nessie, that monster in Loch Ness nobody can prove exists. I pour the wheat-colored cream over Howie's toast. I say to him, "Why don't you have some of this first?"

Howie eats hungrily; he mops the eggs with bread; he breathes hard through his nose. Dominique looks at him, then me, smiling wryly. Bill goes over to the glass slider, pulls it to one side and steps out onto the deck. He's not having breakfast.

* * *

IT IS MID-MORNING.

Bill and I sit in the dinghy, looking for his bird. Marsh grass holds the dinghy perfectly still, captive in the glade. The light is weak, and the sea is smooth. Bill has his binoculars at his side, at the bottom of the dinghy. We have been here forever.

"Nessie, do you love me?" he asks.

I am silent longer than I want to be, but just as silent as I have always been when he asks me this: he always asks me this when he wants to tell me something terrible.

So I say, as I always say, "Why do you ask?"

"Just tell me if you love me, that's all."

"Yes, I love you, Bill; now, what is it?"

Bill is not looking at me. He turns his gaze back to the glade.

"One man I shot in Nam, I shot in a place like this—I told you before. Do you remember?"

"Yes."

Bill rises in the dinghy; he stands, steadying the boat with his knees, which seems impossible; his knees are so insubstantial, his legs so withered. He raises the glasses to his face. The dinghy begins to swing from side to side in greater oscillations.

"I shot this man twice because I didn't shoot him right the first time," Bill says.

"You didn't shoot him *right?*"

Bill speaks down at me, never removing the binoculars from his eyes.

"I had to shoot him twice, that's all. You have a problem with that?"

I never tell Bill I have a problem with things. I leave him with the last question, as always, or I ask him something back.

"What about company? Don't you think Howie and Dom will miss us?"

Bill lets the glasses hang at his chest awhile. Then he removes them and reaches down to hand them to me.

"Screw them," he says—and the dinghy capsizes.

We are in the water, up to our abdomens instantly, so quickly that no amount of thought can reconstruct the swift and unexpected motions that put us there. The dinghy is overturned, floating hull-up.

Bill turns to me briefly; his eyes are huge and wild with fright; they are cold, mackerel eyes, only not the same as a mackerel's; they are bulbous, grotesque with fear.

I say, "Bill, it's okay!"

But I am too late. Bill is slogging his way to shore. I right the dinghy and lift myself over the gunnels into it. I find one of the oars floating nearby and paddle the swamped boat through the seagrass back to the beach house.

* * *

I'M CLEARING THE breakfast dishes, doing math in my head:

Now minus Nam: '87 minus '75…

I tell Bill, "The War's over. Twelve years."

Bill is leaning against the sink, holding a water glass at his side. His mouth is frozen open, eyes bulging.

Bill goes to bed. It's not so amazing anymore. It's just how I think of him, even when we have company. In bed.

I put on the television and go into the kitchen to shell shrimp for the next day. Dom comes in to help. I tell her it's okay. I'm only making enough for Bill and me. She asks me about Bill. I tell her he went back to bed. She understands. That's the hell of it, she and Howie understand.

* * *

BILL SLEEPS THE rest of the morning and part of the afternoon.

And he sleeps now. The others don't mention it. Howie watches the Braves game; he picks over a bowl of popcorn; he sets the bowl in his lap, salts it and shakes it, bringing the unexploded kernels to the top. He bites into the hard kernels until I hear the shells crack. Something gives. Something always gives.

I hear the banter of the television behind me, and nothing from the room where Bill sleeps, only the tide through the partially open French slider growing stronger with each advance of surf. I think about how I never want to leave this place. How I need it. I think again of Bill sleeping in the next room, then hear the anchorwoman talking on the television, the evening news. Her voice moves quickly, easily through the air.

"And in other news tonight, the last known Dusky Seaside Sparrow died today, alone, in a cage…"

* * *

HOWIE, DOM, AND I are playing cards.

But I'm not concentrating. I am thinking about Bill's dead sparrow. I am thinking how I want to take the carcass of the last specimen—the one in the institute—and dismantle it eye by eye, feather by feather, bone by bone. I want to arrange its parts in front of Bill, on the card table; I want to show him that these bits of bird are indiscernible from those of its closest relative. Would one thing be made right if this bird were still alive? Eye for eye, bone for bone, sparrow for sparrow, would it somehow lessen Bill's indecipherable sorrow?

* * *

(NOW THAT THE bird is dead, I guess it doesn't matter.

I am not sure I should tell Bill. Howie doesn't notice the news about it. Thank God.)

Howie and Dom are walking on the beach.

I find Bill sleeping on the couch.

I sit on the carpet and put my arms around him. When we are alone in the beach house, Bill and I sleep a lot in the middle of the day. Just like this. Nap time. Nessie and Bill time. Holy Nessie and Bill time. No one can come in now. Nessie and Bill, forever. We sleep with the nattering of the television and the groping surf covering it over with good words: *things always come around to being fine.*

* * *

DOMINIQUE HELPS ME load the dishwasher.

She says, "How are you and Bill doing?"

I say, "We're okay. Bill wants us to keep the beach house. He's looking for another teaching job."

Dom looks at me like what I have said is impossible. She gives me her *poor thing* look. So I say, "I know we can't afford this place much longer, but you only live once."

That is all Dom and I say: that is all Dom and I ever seem to talk about since Bill and Howie are the only true friends in our foursome. They have the War in common.

We're fine, Dom. It always comes back to that. Being fine.

"So now you know," Dom says, drying her hands with a dishtowel. She's back at the table running her thumbnail along a seam in the wood.

"Now I know what?"

"Now you know Howie's new obsession."

"What's that?" I am ready to laugh because I know it's coming, but I am restrained, too, since I know what Dom has to say will be funny only in the way that things are funny in situations, only laughable if you have a sense of the whole thing.

"Howie's in the stock market again."

"God help us," I say.

"Yeah," Dom says through a sleepy line on her face— a near-smile, "God help us all."

* * *

THE OTHERS ARE sleeping in the front room with the television on.

It's a funny thing about ignorance and happiness. They seem best combined in the company of friends and television: sleep and television seem to cheer Bill.

Things always come back to being fine. With Bill and Howie and Dom, here in the beach house, my notion of what is dark, often torrid, like the crawling sea, comes into the light of day, light of being, light of one day to the next without any current cares. We have no current cares.

God, it's dark, except for the television.

* * *

THE OTHERS ARE awake.

I am thinking and smiling with them. I don't know what we are all talking about. But I am thinking, Bill will get the teaching job. He always does. That's a matter of time. It always is.

* * *

HOWIE IS BUILDING a bonfire on the beach.

Dom packs clams and chicken in cooking pails.

I see Bill at the sink with the water glass again. He refills the glass; I notice once more how thin and drawn his legs are; his knees seem nonexistent—he walks slowly, unsurely, on what seems like two white pegs—they grow paler, woodier each day.

"You sure you don't want anything to eat?" I ask him.

He stands with the water glass pursed to his lips like he might answer me about the eggs. He finishes the water. He never answers me.

Dom stops filling the pails for a moment to watch Howie hurling driftwood onto the towering blaze. "God help us now," she says, shaking her head.

* * *

THE OTHERS ARE on the beach.

I watch the blaze Howie has going, the gigantic shadows he and Dom cast over the sand in the firelight.

Bill is on the couch, where he sits in the unsure, switching light of the television screen. Bill watches television for a long time. I watch it from the kitchen. The bonfire is left to go to embers. Now I watch the fire die until it is only a point of light, an orange, waning light in the dark. I can't see Howie or Dom anywhere on the beach. I load the dishwasher.

The tide is up, and the evidence of the water breaking on the beach is only in sound, not thought: a tearing of the fabric of water, a kind of groan as it comes back together and runs back out, like making love when you are very young, doing it like your life depends on it.

* * *

IT IS LATE, past 3 a.m.

I am standing at the window watching another freighter, or maybe a cruise ship, on the horizon. This one is very far out. It appears to be a weak star. Maybe it is. I don't know how close stars can come to the horizon before they disappear altogether. I don't see any stars around this one, none that close to it. It must be a ship. I don't know if it's moving.

* * *

THIS MORNING, THE sky is partly overcast.

Not rain clouds, just white rags that gauze the sky from horizon to horizon.

Bill sets the oars in the locks and swings them inside the boat. He reaches into a grocery sack, pulls a beer from the plastic ring, and hands it to me. Then he hangs the binoculars around his neck and leans back in the bow of the boat.

He takes the oars and begins rowing.

I have my hand gliding in the pea-green water. Bill pulls in the oars, takes a beer from the sack, opens it, and sips it as we drift north with the wind, away from long grass and scrub stands, out to sea.

I close my eyes; I feel the drift.

Bill takes up the oars again, dips them into the water, and rows us in closer to shore; we approach the grasses. Bill drops the oars and takes up the binoculars. He holds them up to his eyes and gazes over the glade; then, as if he is satisfied he has gauged the distance we need to travel, the place he is making for, he takes the oars back up and moves us closer-in.

"Compared to other sparrows," Bill says, pulling hard on the oars, "this sparrow is supposed to have dark black streaks on its throat and spots on its stomach."

Bill hands me the binoculars and I look through them. I see endless stands of grass. As I look nearer shore, I see scrub bushes with wiry black branches and small green buds tumoring the limbs. Birds, like huge flecks of pepper, scatter from one bush, soar a few seconds, then light on another. These birds have no song. There is only this leaping, soaring game. Suddenly, there are thousands of sparrows, but I see none which strikes me as darker than the next.

Grass whips the belly of the dinghy; I hand the glasses to Bill, who sets them in the bottom of the hull, and pulls back on the oars with more force than before to move us through the glade.

* * *

WE ARE SURROUNDED by broad blades of grass standing out of the water like long knives.

Bill takes up the binoculars.

"I can't see a damn thing," he says.

He rows a short distance into the thickest part of the grass, then stops; the dinghy rocks slightly on the water; there are weeds all around us, nothing in sight but green blades. Bill looks through the glasses again.

"Do you suppose if you were this sparrow—let's say you were the last one on Earth—could you actually *know* you were the last one?"

"I don't know, Bill. Do you see anything?"

He puts the glasses down.

"No," he says.

Bill sips on another beer. He lies his head back. I see his eyes follow the clouds, the way the whole linen mass above moves with the wind, steadily shearing the space between Earth and sky.

He closes his eyes.

"I heard once that the first two people came out of the sea," he says. "They crawled up from the bottom of the sea on a blade of grass, like one of these."

"I never heard that."

"I heard it in the War."

"Oh, maybe that's why," I tell him.

I see the clouds breaking up overhead. A stiff breeze comes over us like the heel of a hand and bends the seagrass to one side. Wind takes the dinghy, turns it, and pushes it out to open water. I close my eyes again to feel the drift. I wonder if the others can see us this far out. How do I tell him the sparrow has perished?

I am waiting for the conversation to end altogether.

I am thinking of a way to get us back to shore.

TWO DIMES

EVEN ILL, HIS mother was a kind woman, and for a time her kindness was part of her illness, the worst of it a $5,000 draft she gave to a man who told her his house had burned "clean to the ground." The house never existed. Man vanished. So did her money. "I felt sorry for him," she told her son on the telephone, and later, "Oh my God, his name? I don't remember," and after that, when she briefly realized the man had swindled her, "I'm going to get it back."

"What," her son groaned, "the money?"

"No, stupid," she replied, "my life."

The weekend after she lost the $5,000, he completed the six-hour drive to her small two-bedroom house in McKeesport. It rained the whole way on the interstate. His radio chattered nervously. Tires from cars ahead of him threw an inky black liquid onto his headlights. He stopped several times at roadside rests to wipe them off, but the black water kept coating them. So, when he pulled into her drive, he felt blinded by the road, looking into relative darkness most of the way. She snapped on the porch light, her robed figure hovering behind the mesh screen door. His eyes ached, head throbbed, and when he stepped into the living room, she brought the full force of three new lamps to bear. He stuck the side of one hand to his brow, squinting at her, eyes adjusting a bit more to the glare. All three lamps were antique brass with frosted globes depicting three stages of young Abraham Lincoln's life, one in his birth cabin, etched HODGENVILLE, KY; another his wielding an axe over a sizable length of timber, reading RAIL SPLITTER; and the third his handing two pennies to a woman possessing a surprised and approving smile—HONEST ABE, of course.

He looked for other obvious loot in the living room, laughing a little with relief when he saw a new purchase on the telephone stand, special-order embossed stationery, KEEP THE FAITH, $100, plus $10.95 shipping and handling—handling by whom?—and what had these so-called handlers thought about what she'd embossed it with?

When his mother entered the room, she sat on the sofa, smiling sweetly, hands placed placidly in her lap, knees together, caps showing white a little above the surface of the coffee table. He winced, seeing opals in all settings imaginable scattered over the coffee table, carelessly as stones in a desert. When he leaned over to inspect the stones, she was right at his elbow, whispering in his ear. "They change with my moods." She wrung her hands, plucked up a particularly brilliant green-blue stone set in a silver brooch. When he saw the bill for the lot underneath, he panicked: $2,597, including fees for inscriptions on all the settings, STONE LOVE, some in script so minuscule he could scarcely read it—but he knew her kind of words. That kind of faith. Her kind of faith.

"We can't afford all this stuff," he told her. He scooped up the opals and receipt off the coffee table and put them in his coat pockets. "What are we going to do?"

She got up from the sofa, came over to him, and leaned in so close he could feel the wisp of her breath on his cheek.

"Never mind that." She patted his coat pocket. "You ever find those two dimes?"

She silenced him, knocked him back, while the memory of two lost dimes piled in his mind. He was nine years old. She'd given him two nice new dimes for ice cream, a miracle since they'd never had that kind of money to spare. She asked him to go a block over and buy orange push-ups for the both of them. As he exited the apartment complex, he could hear the tinny, reverberant bells of the ice cream truck going through the complex. He remembered heading for the sound. He spotted the truck, approached it, then spotted Nicky, a fat kid with a foul odor and elephant-skin elbows, one of those kids with an evil charismatic smirk better-suited to Sean Connery's James Bond than a fat kid. Once, he'd watched Nicky rob another kid while he stood waiting for the ice cream truck. A whole quarter. So when Nicky walked up, he turned his back to the fat boy and popped the two dimes in his mouth.

"Hey, punk!" Nicky said. "What you got in your mouth?"

He turned to face his nemesis, but before he could reply, his panic reflex forced him to swallow both dimes. Nicky stared at him with like panic, a queer expression of wonder and fear—and then Nicky fled, the ice cream truck rolled up, and the driver leaned out the little window.

"What'll it be, kid?" the driver asked, but he'd already taken off, across the street and into the honeycomb of apartments.

How could he explain the incident to his mother? He resolved to tell her any story except the awkward truth. Perhaps he'd say how the ice cream truck nearly careened into a nearby hydrant and, in his excitement, the dimes flew out of his fist and vanished into a sewer grating—or how he saw a man with no legs sitting squarely on the cement holding a sign, POOR AND BLIND, and how, out of compassion, he dropped the two dimes into his cup. But when he came into the apartment, when he saw her waiting patiently for her orange push-up, kindness blooming from her smile, he couldn't help himself.

"I accidentally swallowed them," he told her.

She laughed, then briefly covered her mouth with a hand. "Well, son," she said, "why did you put them in your mouth in the first place?"

"I don't know," he said, thinking not so much about his reason for putting the two dimes there, since that was painfully apparent to him, but thinking how he might die of dime poisoning or some such thing. "I'm going to die, Mom, aren't I?" he added, which also struck him as a splendid diversionary question to get her feeling sorry for him.

"You're not going to die," she replied. "Those dimes will go right through you and end up—you know."

"There?"

"Yes, you must keep checking for them."

For a time, he undertook the awful task of searching for the dimes. He never found them.

He swallowed once, just thinking about the dimes after all this time, a reflex he'd come to expect over the years, but he swallowed harder when he noticed his mother's new pipe organ, tucked unobtrusively in a far corner of the small living room, and swallowed twice more when he finally got her to show him the bill for $15,196 with tax, special freight, handling, and the ten-year extended in-home tuning and warranty.

He scanned the bill feverishly.

"We have to return this!" he said.

She went over to the organ, flipped up the keyboard cover, and began to hammer out "Amazing Grace," complete with vocal accompaniment, THAT SAVED A WRETCH LIKE ME, though he scarcely attended to the tune, her favorite since, as she declared mid-note, muscle under her left eye quivering, "Who needs another song when one has this one?"

* * *

FOUR A.M.—HE knew it because he was staring at the red digits on the dresser when he smelled smoke, just a hint, enough to propel him to his bedroom door, down the hall and into his mother's living room, where he saw her standing over a small fire on the coffee table, flickering shadows reflecting in her face wave after wave of undulating calm. She held his dead father's fake sheepskin hunting coat to her chest. He punched up 911, took the sheepskin coat, tried to beat the flames, and when the fire department arrived, they finished the job with water. A great expanse of wet ash and debris stretched between his mother and him, and at its center stood the remains of the scorched sofa and coffee table scattered with charred gunstocks, a bolt, a couple rifle barrels. He realized she'd piled her dead husband's gun collection on the coffee table, doused it in lighter fluid, and lit it up.

As he crossed the burned room, he could feel wet ashes squish under his bare feet. At his sides, drapes drooped heavily like dark wet cliffs, but he kept his eyes dead on her: Her hair was damp and ropy, like strands of seaweed, but not from the room's drenching. She had a waterproof radio hooked about her right wrist, emblazoned with SING IN THE SHOWER, complete with tiny flourishes of quarter-notes rising skyward. A strange fear grew in him that she had always, secretly, been a mermaid and might dive straight into water puddled at her feet and he'd never see her again. A smiled ticked at one side of his mouth. Then, the Fire Chief—a boyish face framed in a rubber suit stretched over his ears, chin, and forehead—motioned him outside to the porch. The Fire Chief leaned on a porch post, and started swaying back and forth—forth to look down her street for someone else to arrive, then back to peer into her picture window to check on her.

"Look," the Fire Chief said, "about a third of the living room's burned. You're going to have to get her over to the psychiatric ward at the hospital."

"And if I don't?" he replied automatically, not entirely believing his resistance.

"They're on their way," the Fire Chief said in time with a sway towards the picture window. "They're going to arrest her."

When he and the Fire Chief went inside, she was sitting on the pipe organ bench in her purple robe, her cheap sheepskin coat over her lap, its fake wool lining sticking up, singed, the way marshmallows looked after one passed them over a campfire flame.

She then looked at the Fire Chief and nodded at the sheepskin coat in her lap.

"He whapped it with this but good," she said. "He almost had it out."

"We have to go," her son told her and went to his room to dress.

When he returned, he took her elbow and helped her up from the organ bench.

She clutched her fake sheepskin coat and headed for the front door with him. He knew he ought to be figuring out how to help her, but all he could think about was how the fire had spared the pipe organ. It was perfect, and he got goosebumps thinking about how she'd been mashing out "Amazing Grace" only hours before. Amazing, indeed. He would try to return the organ to the store.

"Where to?" she said when they reached her front door.

"The hospital," he said, but before he could finish by saying he'd come to get her things later, she interrupted him, speaking the way people speak when they want to drown something, to wipe it out entirely.

"Well?" she said.

"Well, what?"

"Maybe you don't want your dimes back. But I want mine!"

He shouldn't have been surprised, but the flesh crawled up his neck, not out of fear or worry, but like a tide of memories, of times when she could be kind without being crazy, of times when he belonged to her, followed her, was so much at peace in her presence, no more so than when she was in her kitchen, showing him the fine art of kneading flour into dough, dough into pie crust, cutting apples into filling.

"Pat the butter on top," she warned. "Never spread it."

Her ways were beyond economy. She strained hot bacon grease through old hand towels with grace; collected bread crusts with aplomb; pickled watermelon rinds to perfection; and created from scratch a glassware collection from used jam jars, bright, clean, beautifully arranged in a three-tier pyramid on her counter.

This was how he wanted his mother to be: frugal, wise, magical. Not like this. He cringed a little, hoping she really didn't expect him to come up with her dimes. He unhooked the shower radio from her wrist and pretended to try to tune to the news. She didn't say anything else while he drove her to the hospital, just picked tiny charred balls of polyester out of her fake sheepskin coat and kept flicking them at him, trying to get one inside his right ear. Once, she made it and laughed. He dug the tiny ball of burned polyester out of his ear and flicked it back at her.

Someone from the police department had called ahead to the hospital. When they arrived, she sat opposite the reception desk on a long, padded bench. She took out the pocket watch her dead husband had given her to time things in the kitchen, inscribed WORLD'S GREATEST COOK, 1965. She held it to one ear, presumably to ascertain whether it was ticking, and then held it to the other ear. Why only 1965? He wondered. Why not WORLD'S GREATEST now? Two times, was all he could think. Two dimes. Two times. Two dimes times two. Jesus—she'd done it to him again: The more he tried to think seriously about the enormity of her spending and situation, the more he kept monkeying around in his mind about the two dimes—small change. Then, he thought it may be natural for someone to think about trivial things when they had important things to think about, like a path of least resistance, fluid and fast, like the path he wished the dimes had taken through his body—the path to discovery and victory. Yes, she'd done it to him again. The dimes discombobulated him. And now, of all times. He could hardly keep his mind on the litany of questions the hospital receptionist was asking him to get the paperwork filled out. His mind flew. And when he looked back to check on his mother, seeing her stick the pocket watch to one ear then the other, he almost envied her. Such peace that passeth understanding.

He was nervous. "May I have a private room?" he asked the receptionist, who was by then busy scribbling his mother's social security number on a form.

"For you?" she said.

"No," he smiled. "Her."

"You're lucky."

The receptionist glanced at his mother, who was grimacing, trying to twist the stem of the pocket watch.

"I am?" he asked.

"Yes—we have one private, but only for a couple days." Then she added, "Insurance?"

"I don't know. I have to go through her things at the house."

When the attendant arrived to escort her back into the psychiatric ward, she handed the pocket watch to him. "I don't know if it's wound or not," she said. "Would you wind it?" The attendant wound it and handed it back to her. "Thank you," she said. She pulled her fake sheepskin coat snug about her, took the attendant's arm warmly, then handed the watch back to the attendant. "Keep it," she said.

* * *

HE SEARCHED HER house most of that evening for some sign of her medical insurance, came up with nothing, got a couple hours of sleep in damp smoky air, woke. He could feel the panic rise in him to a mysterious high mark, pictured her smiling, handing her pocket watch to the attendant. Her damned kind smile. Then, he noticed a small note taped to the wall over the pipe organ: the groundhog, Punxsutawney Phil, his first look out of his hole in months, the big question looming—how much more winter would one need to bear?—and the caption below, CARPE DIEM. Through it all, her odd sense of humor remained, as if some profound ordering intelligence were at work, twos in tension—tragedy and comedy, irrationality and harmony, mother and son. Twos in tension he'd sensed in nature. Night and day; breathing in and out.

She was no earth-mother, to be sure, but something, he was sure, guided things she did, even her most annoying little habits. But what was it? What? What, indeed!

He was doing it again, thinking of the two dimes. Round and round they turned in his head—was it possible for two coins to remain inside his body for decades? Perhaps some obscure gland of his had excreted a strange coating on them, like something in a horror flick, and any time now, two conjoined dimes would crawl out of his throat, a living monster of metal and blood, ready to shock the world. He was sure he hadn't passed the dimes. Damn her—he supposed it was nice to have this sort of trivial distraction to think about in the face of having to commit her for psychiatric care, but he might have hoped for some less disgusting one.

In the morning, he drove to the mall to see about returning the pipe organ to the music store. When he entered the store, he was met by the manager, a man with glassy eyes and a whip-moustache the shape of swept-back nostrils of a snake. The man looked evil. It was too coincidental. He couldn't possibly be evil. But he looked so evil, it was funny, and the man's evil appearance gave him new hope. With all the forces against coincidence on his side, no way this snakish man could be a vile, heartless materialist. He'd get the refund. She needed it for medical expenses. Besides, it was so peaceful in the store, no one around, the other organs looking like large ships of maple, cherry, and oak sitting at all orientations to one another, like big beautiful boats, all in safe harbor. He navigated through the showroom toward old Snake Stache, through carpeted canals between bright glossy pipe organs, noticing the same sign in gold block letters over the pricier models, HOW SWEET THE SOUND.

When he reached Snake Stache, he hadn't expected to open himself up to him, but planned to lie, to say that his mother'd been diagnosed with Parkinson's disease and obviously could not play the organ she'd purchased—or that she found the reverberation not quite right—or? The moment of truth was at hand. He steeled himself to tell the good lie, something he believed would sit well with any reasonable person, elicit, with a tell-tale human wag of the head, condescension, pity, and approval.

But in the end, he said, "My mother was not in her right mind when she bought the organ. Surely, I can return it. Her husband's just died. She really needs the money."

Snake Stache shook his head and smiled. Seeing that smile, his heart leapt and FIFTEEN GRAND flashed in his mind.

"Sorry," Snake Stache said, "sales are final on big-ticket items like that."

He felt himself go suddenly dark inside, not from his momentary lapse in judgment— speaking the truth—but from something else: Wasn't his mother a big-ticket item herself?

"Look," he said to the man, advancing on him a couple of steps, "what good is your commission if you have to get it this way? What kind of—" He could see the man's glassy eyes light a little with fear, so he gained control of himself and leaned back on the cold keyboard cover of an organ to let his anger subside. When he came forward again, he could see Snake Stache lean back, anticipating a reprisal—and he gave him one. "Here," he said, reaching into his pocket and sorting through a handful of change. He plucked a dime from the little pile of change, inspected it briefly—LIBERTY, 'P' for PHILADELPHIA—then picked out another dime. He hurled the two dimes at the man, one of which hit him edgewise, high in the delicate bridge of his nose, causing him to seize his snout with two fingers the way one does when eating ice cream seems to freeze one's brain. "There's a bonus, asshole," he added, just as Snake Stache reached down with his free hand to collect blood dripping out one nostril.

When he left the mall, he drove around awhile. He wondered how one thin dime could cause Snake Stache's nose to bleed. He must have really zinged him. Hit him just right. After a time, he found himself near the river— he didn't know which: Allegheny, Monongahela, it didn't matter. He parked at a long stretch of riverbank where, long ago, his father had taken him and his mother to swim. The river was low, calm, vacant. But from those old times, he remembered bright varnished speedboats in the river, their propellers roiling water high, so high he imagined it standing higher than its logical surface, a buoyant and beautiful convex meniscus, a mighty feeling, the power of water and memory that seemed to emanate from somewhere in his lower chest—from a spot where the dimes had gotten stuck? No—it wasn't anything to do with the dimes; it had to do with high-water marks painted white on dark concrete bridge pilings, and words, FIFTEEN FEET—and water, so much water, and memory. Even after the wakes of the speedboats subsided, the river sloshed high against its banks, so high it seemed that then—and now—it stuck in his throat. What water! —even ill, there was a kindness and a humor in his mother, full and round and spanning so much time. When he left the river, he took its highest parts with him, memories, his spirit soaring with its indescribable brim swell.

* * *

FOR SOME REASON, he'd expected her doctor to be a very young man like the Fire Chief. But when he met him the next morning, the doctor looked to be in his sixties. He had a tidy desk, his mother's file in front of him, all sorts of notes scribbled on the inside flap. The man had an oval, friendly face, and though an old face, it was at the same time youthful and pensive, like that of a choir boy's. He wondered if the doctor might know how to play the piano—or pipe organ—or sing in church, he mused, another instance of how his mother'd infected him with her crazy whimsy. Then he noticed the doctor's fingertips, all ten bandaged with white adhesive tape.

"Cancer," the doctor said in a tone one might say 'Hello' when answering the telephone. "Benign." The doctor tapped his white fingertips on his desk, then paged through his mother's file. "Before you see your mother," he said, "I want you to know that she's on medication. It seems to be working. But she may say some off-beat things. Don't worry. It's normal."

Normal? Worry? Why should he worry? His mother had always been his mother, would always be. She was the original article, the one and the same, the alpha and the omega, the invisible eye of the dust devil as it now watched him spinning about her in a cloud of debris. And if she was ill, well, it had to be a change in a sea that was yet her sea. Even when the doctor rose to show him to her room, he was going through everything in his mind. "You ever pass those two dimes?" Indeed. She couldn't disarm him anymore. He was on to her. He liked being disarmed. He liked her. The idea of her. He always had—in the dim past, he had followed her with fascination through every room of their apartment, into every closet, drawer, anywhere she might keep things that might help him decipher her. She couldn't turn him against her, no matter how hard she tried. She was his life's work. He only had to see her, to tell her he'd had a vision of the river rising, and of her and her husband, and that he understood—at least a little, at least enough. He knew she was bearing up, keeping the faith, depressed about her husband's death. Sure, for a time, things sloshed around in confusion, but then they rose to some unimaginable high point. They settled, calmed. Everything would come around.

When he entered her room, she was sitting up on the bed, her chin resting on her chest, a little flesh rolled up around her neck, eyes closed, asleep.

"Mom," he said.

He stood at the door a short while, noticed the on-duty nurse's name, ROSIE, in pink chalk on a green slate, and below that, MEDS 2 PM. When his mother opened her eyes, she rose automatically, turned and sat on the edge of the bed. Her hair was beautiful the way it framed her face. The tick under her left eye was gone, but seeing the stony look on her face, he almost wished it would return. She was looking straight ahead, not at him, somewhere out the tiny window, and he found himself looking around the room. He wanted something of hers to take home with him. He peered inside her bathroom, only to find another sign above the toilet, PULL FOR EMERGENCY. There was only her singed sheepskin coat draped over the back of a stick chair near the window. He found another chair and dragged it next to her bed. He rested his elbows on his knees and leaned a little forward, feeling embarrassed because his posture seemed rather like he was inspecting the bridge over the river, not his mother. Repulsed by his own insensitivity, he reached out and pressed his palm to her forehead. Almost immediately, her face wrinkled, and she began to sob. He removed his hand from her forehead. She stopped sobbing. His urge—who wouldn't have had such an urge?—was to press his hand against her forehead again to see if she'd sob, and then to see if applying slightly more pressure with his palm would stop her sobbing. But before he could try it, she turned to him. She smiled. He spotted another curious sign above her telephone, HOW TO DIAL OUT.

A nurse's assistant wheeled in a tray of food. His mother refused and asked that the tray be set in front of him. He shook his head, but eventually gave in, prodding at a pale gray square of meatloaf. His mother pointed her finger at the bit of meat.

"You gonna eat that?"

"Yes," he said—and then he didn't eat it.

"Bad for the digestion, anyway." She smiled thinly. "By the way, did you say you passed those two dimes?"

There, he thought. He'd make the miniscule matter of his passing the two dimes enormous; he would give her what she wanted, try it her way, make the two dimes brave and prodigious, overflowing like the river he remembered.

"I found the dimes," he said. "I threw them at the music store manager. You should have seen him bleed out his nose."

His mother turned and looked at him. She grinned a little. He grinned back at her. Then she rose, walked to the chair by the window, picked up the fake sheepskin coat, and hurled it at his head, where it landed, enclosing him in darkness.

"You stupid bastard," she said, her voice seeming far off in a distant corner of the room. "I'm broke. No insurance. Hospital bills. And you go throwing money away?"

He wasn't sure how long he sat with the coat over his head. When he dragged it off his face, she was asleep in bed, the light low. He left her room quietly. He entered the hallway. He drove the entire six hours home before realizing he'd taken her burned fake sheepskin coat with him. Once home, before getting into bed, he dressed the coat over his shoulders and stood in front of the mirror. He was grinning again, grinning until his grin became new knowledge of where the two dimes had gotten to, not stuck in some dark lavender fold of his intestines, not in the brim-tide of unconditional love, but dissolved in his blood, coursing in veins, two dimes that were no longer hers and his, but two dimes that had become one thing, a new world of metal and blood, the life-liquid of the monster emerged, a single feeling that overcame him suddenly—a mere twenty cents.

THE HERMITAGE, 2:10 P.M.

But there is a meaning? A meaning? …
Look, it's snowing. What meaning has that?
—Chekhov, *The Three Sisters*

MY ROOMMATE SMITH just sat there, looking up at me, like he expected me to say something more. He was not like himself. Shy Smith. Unselfconsciously conscious Smith. Smith of Smiths. Broke Smith. Absolutely flat-busted, FAFSA student-loaned to the yin and yang Smith. If he tried, Smith couldn't pay his student loans back in two lifetimes. He was a history major and a troubled boy with dark circles around his eyes. He could barely afford to be diabetic. He sat on his bed with his back flat against the cinderblock wall. He looked gaunt, beat-out, the usual for Smith, but he also looked snug and serene, too.

I was feeling pretty good, a glow on, beginning to feel the dark beer. I was in the best state possible, confined to our room in a snowstorm, feeling perfect since it was Friday night, a long stretch to Monday classes, and since Smith hadn't had a drink all night. He bragged he could be straight about things, while I was buzzed, jaded, and it was fine by me, so long as I wouldn't have to worry about Smith slipping into a coma.

Smith listened to me talk, watched me pace the room back and forth, wall to wall, like a slow pendulum in the housing of a ridiculous clock.

So, even if he wasn't loaded, I said, "We'll just have to make the best of it. Look at it this way. In this weather, no one's going to bother us."

I carried my bottle of dark beer and wandered the room, knocking into one object then another: two twin beds with vintage mattresses, one of two small matching dressers, two desks, and four stick chairs. I went over and stripped the blanket from my bed. I wrapped it around myself. I pinned the blanket with one hand at my neck and continued to drink my beer with the other hand. I got up from the bed and started pacing again. Tick. Tock.

Smith rubbed his back up and down against the cinderblocks.

"Yeah," he said, "you look relaxed."

"I'm going to Russia when I get out of here," he declared. "Maybe for good."

Smith had been going on about Moscow and whatnot all night.

"Damn it, Smith," I said, feeling woozy, "why don't you give it a rest?" Smith wasn't listening. I went on. "What's the difference, anyway? If you're going to Russia to get away from things here, forget it. The big-ticket item in Moscow is the Big Mac. The Combo. It's progress."

Smith reached for something on the floor, got up from bed, and stood in front of me. His face was obscured by black—click!—pop!—light exploded in the room; then, circles of light crested like waves; an orange dot was stuck in the air like a tiny ripe setting sun; it bounced and wobbled; it grew a tail of light and swung back and forth; my eyes hurt.

"I'm blinded, you son of a bitch," I told him.

"There," Smith said and put his camera back on his bed, "now you won't be forgotten."

The orange ball hung in the room a long while, stubborn, and after it died, I got my glow back from the dark beer. Give it a rest, I thought. For chrissake, Smith!

That was when Smith brought Luba's pics of Russia up on my "El Cheapo" Gateway student laptop, the sort one wants often to slap shut like a rotten sandwich and toss into the snow. Luba lived in the east wing of the complex. She had grandparents in Ukraine. She was really fat, but she liked Smith, so she sent him the pics. Smith knew she liked him, but he ignored her. The more he ignored her, the more she tried to please him. It was humiliating. I was glad she was in New York for the weekend.

Smith rifled through his desk and came out with a crinkled paper, Luba's notes that went with her pictures.

He opened a bottle of dark beer, poured some into a small tumbler, and handed it to me.

"How you feeling?" he asked me, like he wanted to be sure I was sober enough to look at the pics.

I told him, "Okay." I suckled at the tumbler. "Thanks for the beerski," I said.

"You want to look at these snaps?"

I couldn't have cared less about Smith's pics of Russia. Besides, I was already feeling okay, so I didn't want anything to spoil my glow. But I didn't tell Smith this. It wasn't that I wanted to spare Smith's feelings. I just didn't know how to explain the glow to him, how strange and delicate the feeling was, like a silken sleep, like a web heavy with dew, about to break, about to be broken by Smith's pics. I felt a little ridiculous thinking about how I couldn't explain things to him, so I let him go on with his picture show.

He sat up in bed, rested the Gateway in his lap, clicking through the snaps, coddling the screen, at times picking up the PC and cocking it sideways for me to see. I was standing and sipping the dark beer, slow and easy so I wouldn't accelerate the evenness of my buzz. Smith started clicking through the pics faster, then he slowed, and slowed even more when he came to the shots of Saint Petersburg.

"Leningrad," he said adoringly.

"Saint Petersburg," I said.

"Leningrad," he insisted.

"What the fuck," I said. "Leningrad."

It was somewhere around Leningrad that I lost what Smith was saying about the pics; then I made an effort.

"Who takes a picture of a map?" I asked, swooping in.

"That's the Kamchatka Peninsula," he said, "the part that looks like a syringe."

"You mean like the name of the vodka?"

"Yeah." He Smith-smiled. "Only your Kamchatka's made in Kentucky."

I settled back and started listening to the wind outside the room and turned to the window. I watched the powdered snow swirl and blast the pane like sand. My mind went off, prodigal-like, a place so far from where we were, walking in a distant province, not part of the same continent. It wasn't that I didn't want my mind to be with me; it had left because of the howling snowstorm. For a parsec, I thought how the snowstorm and cinderblocks felt like me and Smith were in Siberia. Then I thought, Who the fuck cares? A parsec's so small, once you think of it, it passes. I was feeling so good and comfortable to be in the dormitory with Smith in a smooth smear of time, student-broke, no place to go, no place that wanted us, no place we had to be.

I wanted to tell Smith, Go ahead, dream of Russia. I supposed, for guys like Smith, the only way out of the dorm is to imagine your way out, like guys in gulags in the old Soviet days, which made me wonder if gulags still existed somewhere, maybe not even in Russia, like secretly, or semi-secretly, like Guantanamo Bay and such. I imagined Smith in a gulag, walking, wall to wall, bouncing about like a runaway pinball, hoping that, with one swing across the room, this way or that, he'd stagger out of the dull pattern of gulag life. Me, I was happy to stay blitzed until the spring thaw to achieve such a state. There wasn't any use in thinking any further. This thought. That thought. Tick. Tock. This is how my mind worked. By itself, on itself. I mean, part of me hoped Smith wouldn't get that Russia couldn't be any better than here. He might get snockered and slip into unconsciousness. Then I'd have a real a mess on my hands.

I let the blanket fall to the floor, stepped over it, found my Salems on the desk, and lit one up.

"You can't smoke in here," Smith said, automatically rather than accusatorily, so I took a nice long drag and sent it his way in a smooth plume of carcinogens.

Smith turned back to the Gateway and his snapshots of Russia, but as time went on, it was like he knew about the glow I had on, how my head had run away, and how I didn't want to be bothered. He was probably hoping some odd juncture of shape and shadow would capture my attention. I knew he was trying to have me say just once, "Tell me about that one, Smith," or "Where do you suppose Luba shot that?" But I thought, Who cares,

Smith? I knew where I was, firm grip on reality, minus my head, but I still knew I'd be there until spring, same as Smith. We weren't going anywhere, least of all Russia. So why did he go on with the pics?

Then he stopped clicking and straightened himself in his bed. I could see his head had come off, too—the way his eyes seemed lifted and distant.

"You want a diet soda or something?" I asked him. "You up to it, Smith? Hey, Smith. Earth to Smith!"

I don't know. I guess I had just had enough of looking at the cinderblocks, the institutional bone color of the room; I was tired of hearing the steam condensing in the radiator, socking itself against the pipes. Bong, bing. So I became this evil person I sometimes became when I felt free, when I thought I really felt I had a hold of a problem, and felt merciless since I could be so falsely merciful.

"Smith," I said, "you need a break. You want to try hitching rides with me tomorrow?"

Smith didn't answer me. He smiled briefly, like we'd for sure end up as handbags made by some loopy Hannibal Lecter character. I laughed, then I recognized the laugh as my evil laugh, so I quickly took another sip of dark beer, hoping I could keep the glow on, and shut up before Smith found out I was slipping into my evil mood.

I walked over to his bed, and he held the Gateway up. I looked at the pic of Russia and sipped more dark beer. I was rocking a little, so I caught myself and stood straight up.

"What's that?" I asked Smith, partly to divert him from studying my face, and partly because I felt odd, like I was losing my balance.

I took my Gateway from Smith and moved it back and forth in front of my face. This wasn't working, so I paused, moving my eyelids up and down, blotting the beer foam from my mustache with my hand. I rubbed my thumbs into my eyes, and finally got the scene of the pic: the snow was trampled; a gray wet street ran up and down the snapshot, terminating at a river's edge; a huge granite building stood on the right side of the road, not unlike so much architecture I'd seen online called Soviet Brutalism. This building was ornate with curling cornices, lions resting on smooth white slabs, small windows, no people.

Smith's commentary was synchronous with my perusal of the pic:

"When Peter the Great was a boy," he said, "he had them build an enormous boathouse, like a grand tomb. There, he kept a boat the size of a skiff."

The storm was coming up hard, reaching its peak. Wind rattled the glass in the window frame. I put out my cigarette. I didn't know what to say. I scowled at Smith. I mean, it wasn't like I couldn't appreciate the absurdity of little Peter's big boathouse, it was just that I already knew Smith had. We had agreed at the beginning of the semester that we wouldn't waste words with one another when things were already understood.

Smith clicked off the pic of Peter's boathouse.

"Who asked you, anyway?" he said.

He put on his slippers and went down the hall to take a whiz. I could feel the glow I had go heavy in my head, calling it back from distant places, like gas cooling and seeking ground zero—sinking. My head was spongy, and thoughts were trickling down inside me. I didn't dare sit down or lie back on the bed—but there was this evil in me that kept me going. I was standing there lock-kneed so I wouldn't keel over, swaying a little, side to side.

I lit another cigarette. I decided my mood wasn't the worst sort since Smith already knew about my moods. We had talked about them before. I had given him fair warning: Since he knew about my evil moods, I had told him, it made them less sinister, right?

Smith came back from his whiz.

"You're full of shit," he said with his Smith smile.

I took up the Gateway, clicked ahead to the next pic, and got it into focus.

Smith stood behind me. I heard him rub his beard stubble with his hands.

"That's the prison in Leningrad—there, you see, that tall wall cut off in the picture at the right? Thousands of political prisoners were executed there. When the bodies piled up, they heaved them over the side of the prison wall. The bodies floated out to sea."

I could tell from his voice that Smith was proud of his lurid description; it was not like him. It was getting really creepy—spooky—since I was supposed to be the one with the mysteriously evil moods, not Smith.

"No shit, Smith," I said. "You suppose they tortured college students in there? I mean, like, ones with big-ass loans they couldn't possibly pay back?"

That was all I could say about the pic of the prison at Leningrad. So Smith went back to his bed. He sat on it and rocked. And I was still standing, and then I was prowling again, bed to bed, talking, remembering how glad I was that Smith wasn't buzzed so he could hear all of this straight.

"Look, Smith," I said, "I hope you get to go to Russia and whatnot when you get out of here, and I won't talk about it anymore after now, okay? But you can't live on this kind of thing exclusively. I mean, you can't be thinking about being in Russia all the time you're here. It'll just make you unhappy. Nobody says you have to choose. You couldn't go to Russia even if you wanted to. You don't have any money. No 'cash-port' to travel. And how're you going to afford insulin over there? You'll die. You're stuck here. In the good old USA. So just calm down." I felt my foul mood unapproachable; there was no way to stop it. "God bless America," I added. "Fuck you and Russia."

Smith got up and went over to the radiator by the window. He twisted the round black valve on the top. The steam gushed in, banged once against the pipes, then twice; it knocked softly a couple more times and stopped. Bing. Bong.

"You want another beer?" Smith asked me.

"Yeah, okay," I said, then added, "how are you, Smith? You okay? I mean are you really okay?"

Smith took the cap off the dark beer and handed the bottle to me.

"I don't know. What difference does it make?" he said.

I poured the dark beer into my glass.

"Jesus," I said. "You know what I mean, Smith. You have those black rings around your eyes again. Just forget about that shit I was saying about Russia."

He was eyeing a bottle of dark beer.

"You need to stay off the sauce," I said.

"I don't know," Smith mumbled.

The glow was in my feet now, so I stretched a hand back uneasily for a chair. The chair wasn't there, so I swayed upright, locking my knee joints again. Smith grabbed my laptop and held it my face. It was a picture of a dark palace with many peaks and spires.

"The Hermitage," Smith said. "But it's like Louis the Fourteenth influenced the architect. The Sun King. It's really rich, gold leaf everywhere—everything curls, really curls from the walls, pillars, furniture."

"The Tsar's Winter Palace," I said.

"During the Revolution, the Bolsheviks took the place in a single afternoon."

"Not a hell of a good hermitage," I said.

"Not really," he said and clicked to the next pic. "Here's a shot of Catherine the Great, a full-length portrait."

The pic showed a painting of a farm-faced woman with thin lips. Nobody to speak of since whatever curves she may have possessed were sunk somewhere in billowing silk and ruffles. She had a librarian's eyes, eyes that made me feel guilty, like I had a huge stack of books overdue.

I told Smith that Catherine the Great did not appear to be as great as her reputation. I said I'd rather be making it with the *Mona Lisa*. At least she seemed like the kind of woman who could have a good time and still show some faint recollection in her smile.

Smith got out his smartass camera and popped another pic of me. I felt dizzy and blind. I put my arms out and reached for his throat, but he ducked, and I fell onto my bed. I laughed my evil laugh, watching an orange dot dance under my eyelids, up and down.

"Do that again and I'll clean your clock," I said.

Smith relaxed. He didn't seem to mind my cracks about his pics or my trying to choke him. My biggest fight was to keep my evil mood under control.

Smith wagged his head. "I don't know, man. There's something about Russia. Something."

He went over to the window and felt it with his hand. He said it was a real bitch out. From my bed, I watched him remove his hand from the glass. I watched the steamed outline of his hand fade from the pane. I thought about the stupid pics he'd taken of me. I doubted that either of us would be remembered.

I got up from my bed, swallowed the last bit of dark beer, about a one-inch heel, set the glass back on the desk, and slumped back onto my bed.

"You and goddamned Russia, Smith," I said, and I closed my eyes. My mouth was on automatic, like I was speaking in tongues to him. Between my eyeballs and eyelids there were worms and stars, and ringing in my ears. Ring a ding. "It's a free country," I added. "You do what you want to."

And then, my wagging tongue was still, just like that; it got numb and stopped. The worms and stars were still in a strange interplay behind my eyelids, and it seemed like I could hear the smallest things. I heard Smith's weight load up the springs of his mattress. I heard him get back up, turn off the lights, and lie back down. My glow was all gone. Everything stopped.

*　*　*

LATER THAT NIGHT, Smith woke me. He was sitting on my bed, right at my face with a burning candle. The rings around his eyes were blacker than before and swollen. He held the Gateway at my nose.

"Jesus, Smith," I groaned.

"Look," he whispered, steadying the laptop.

I reached out of the covers and pushed the screen back a little so I could see it better.

"It's a clock," Smith said. "Got it? A mantle clock in the Tsar's Winter Palace."

"Yeah, it's got the same curly gold leaf all over it." I rubbed my eyes. "So what?"

"Right, exactly," Smith said. "Read the time, check out the hands, right there."

"Ten after two," I said. "So the fuck what?"

"Right, two-ten p.m. The clock's broken. Stopped. It's been stuck at ten after two in the afternoon for over a hundred years."

"No shit," I said.

"Right!" Smith seemed elated. "The Bolsheviks broke the clock when they swarmed the Winter Palace, and it's been stuck ever since then, just like that."

Smith was sitting on my leg, so I yanked it out from under him.

"So freaking what, Smith?" I said.

"Well, isn't it incredible? I mean, there's really something to it! You know what I mean?" Smith turned the screen to himself and stared at it. "It is. It's incredible. Everything stopped. Everything changed. Like when the Berlin Wall crumbled. We can never know how incredible. We can never know."

I sat up in bed and flung the covers off myself.

"Why don't you just take it easy?" I said. "Look at me. I've never been so godfuckingdamn content in my life! But every time I get feeling good, you start this Russia crap on me. What do you know about it? What? Nothing! That's what! You never will! Go to sleep!"

Smith stood over my bed and glared at me, then the Gateway, then back at me. He looked like he was going to kill me—or himself. I didn't know which or what to do. So the evil, sympathetic me said, "Hey, Smith, you want a beerski or something?"

He said no and went back to his own bed holding the candle in one hand, still staring at the pic. I asked him again if he wanted a beer, but he just sat staring at the picture, nodding no at me.

"I feel really cooped up in this place," I said. "You want to walk?"

We got our winter gear on and went outdoors. The snowstorm had ebbed, and the night sky was clear, starstrewn. The powder lay still, shining in the way snow shines with bits of blue light, reflecting in moonlight. We made our way out of the dormitories. I remember we sounded like work horses shuffling through the fresh snow, muddling the flat, wide blanket with our boots.

When we were far out across the dark, white expanse, Smith turned to look at the hunkering complex from which we had come. Not one window was lit, not even that of our tiny cinderblock quarters.

"Look, Smith," I said, "all that crap I said before about Russia. I didn't mean it—it was just the black beer talking."

He wasn't listening. He was walking ahead.

"What time is it?" he asked without looking back to me.

"I don't know. I honestly don't," I said. I made a couple quick steps to catch up to him. "You've got a touch of cabin fever, Smith. That's all."

I told him this, but it didn't seem to make a bit of difference, so without a bit of the glow, without the evilness that had been in me, without a smidgen of my usual meanness, I caught him, took his arms, turned him, and faced him to me.

"I know what you're up to, Smith," I said. "You want me to say living here is like living in Russia, all its bloody travails. You want me to connect things."

But "the clock" is all he mumbled.

"This is *not* Russia, Smith!" I said, quickly. "It's *not*!" I said. "Not really. I mean, it's *not*!"

Again he mumbled, "The clock."

"Freaking come on," I said. "Right now," I pleaded softly. "Just be my old Smith in all your Smithyness."

But Smith didn't say a word. Not about Russia. Or Leningrad. Or afternoon revolutions. Or Catherine the Great. Nothing.

He lowered his eyes and looked at the snow.

I looked at his cold, wizened face, eyes sunk into dark pockets in his head, and knew I had failed, that my meanness had come back with all the claustrophobic force of my glow, only now it wasn't a delicate, silken glow, just a leaden throbbing in my head like the dull knocking of a cracked chime. I hit him. I hit him hard on his chest with my fists.

"Say something," I groaned. "For chrissake," I said. "Snap out of it, Smith. For pity's sake!"

HIS MOTHER, FROM A GREAT DISTANCE

OUT OF HER element.

Never flown in her life.

Yet she sets off for the international terminal in Houston, tows a small brown suitcase with tiny brass wheels, clickety clacking over metal strips in composite flooring, pink magnolia-printed dress tightly about her hips, index toes piggyback over big toes that poke out ends of too-small sandals, toenails spackled with deep-red, chipped and sheenless polish, mouth in a tight line of determination, tongue swiping her lower lip, gulping for air.

My foot, she huffs when the TSA man asks her to remove her sandals. His stern look, the one she knows well, so she complies with a fish grin, swims for the gate, as if upstream, stops to ask three different people for directions, boards the plane, argues with a white-haired paisley-tied businessman about which number and letter correspond to the window or aisle seat, which in the long run becomes irrelevant because a gallant college exchange student surrenders his window seat to her.

She snaps her seatbelt buckle into place.

Asks the young man, How far to Vilnius?

* * *

TO HIM IT seems an impossible passage.

All the way from Houston to the Baltic coast of Lithuania, where he works at the Writer's Union in Nida, on the spit dividing the Baltic Sea and Kuršių Marios, the inland lagoon. His quarters are on the hill overlooking the marina, far above the water, a short stroll downhill to the dock, where, on clear days, he can spot the speedboat coming a long way off, coming from Kaunas, out the Nemunas estuary.

He rises from the old Soviet state bed, stretches, goes into the water closet, stands a long time facing the mirror over the sink, then passes to a window.

Breakfast: his diet cola swimming in nearly melted ice; air he breathes in bursts between gulps from the can.

Outside the Writer's Union, the sky clears, and he notices a couple having coffee at the kavinė on the roof. The parking lot, usually full of buses from Germany and Poland, is nearly empty, a lull after the weekend tourist-crush.

He likes it this way, the town dead; he never wants it to change.

SHE'LL TRY EVERY gadget for sure.

Thirty minutes after takeoff, she untangles the cord of the audio headset and, after pressing all the buttons on the armrest and overhead, after two trips by the steward to her seat to ask, Do you need anything, ma'am? and to switch off the call button, she breaks out her complimentary flight kit, requiring the college exchange student to step into the aisle while she wriggles, apologetically, to unbuckle her seatbelt, then, wedging the gray plastic complimentary shoehorn beneath the heel of her excruciatingly constrictive sandals, pops them off one by one, slips on her complimentary Trans-Atlantic comfort socks, and, as the student tries to reseat himself, gallantly, of course, she removes the miniscule bottle of body lotion and massages it into every square centimeter of exposed epidermis until the contents are gone. Then she places the sleeping blindfold over her eyes, settles back, wrings her hands slowly like small pectoral fins sculling water.

* * *

AN OCTOPUS'S GARDEN.

He wants a certain rhythm descending the hill from the Writer's Union, yet gravity pulls at him in canted waves, so he stiffens his pace against the Earth's pull until he reaches the bottom, relaxing, moving slowly along

Taikos Street for the marina, past the Neringa Hospital, walking among arrow-straight exposed roots in shifting sand of the Nida dunes, smoke drifting from pork kebab stands.

He finds a bench located near the water so he can see the marina. Later, he gets up, stands in line at the smoked fish kiosk, where dozens of smoked ungurys—eels—swing by strings tacked to the top edge of the kiosk. Behind the strings stands the eel-woman, striped in light sifting through ungurys' carcasses, shadowed by her Beatles bangs—so she calls them in English, for she's one of only a few who speak English at the marina—Beatles bangs because tapes by the Fab Four were the first she remembers getting smuggled during the Soviet occupation by *knygnešiai*, book smugglers moving through Kalingrad.

My favorite is "Octopus's Garden," she once told him.

He's next in line at the fish kiosk. The eel-woman parts the curtain of dry shivering eels to peer at him, only a sliver of her long, tan face showing like a moray inspecting its surroundings from its craggy den in the deep.

The Sun is high overhead, and a soft, glistening blue sky lingers about the blaze.

Under all, not a single shadow is cast.

Prašau? the eel-woman woman asks, moray-face jutting a little more out the veil of eel carcasses.

Ungurys, he says, proud of his Lithuanian intonation. Vienna.

She rewards his enunciation with a suspicious smile, quickly removes one of the smoked ungurys carcasses from the display, wraps it in a waxed paper bag, and hands it to him. He pays and slips the eel into his satchel.

* * *

IT'S JUST LIKE her to speak with perfect strangers.

By the time they leave the East Coast of the U.S., over the North Atlantic, she raises her blindfold above her eyes, brushes her teeth with the complimentary toothpaste and two-part breakaway toothbrush, spits the gooey residue of saliva and spent paste into her bag reserved for air sickness.

The in-flight feature movie begins, and she speaks straight into the liquid, greenish fluorescent darkness, turning time to time to see that the gallant college exchange student listens.

She says: It would be just like my son to go to Lithuania. It's bad enough once you take babies off your nipple: you start to lose them. But my son was allergic to my milk. Hated the stuff. His eyes swelled shut; he could hardly breathe. He'd bawl and bawl for days. And so only after four weeks, pop! He came right off my breast, you see, too soon…and now he thinks it damaged him—and you combine that with his father never telling him he believed in God and dying so young, well, it's no wonder he turned out to be a writer. My son says writers are damaged. One time, he thanked *me* for damaging him!

* * *

TWO FACES.

The sky above the water of the Marios is a fathomless blue. On his right rise the great dunes of Nida, waves of heat crawling from their fleshy white surfaces like translucent snakes, half-real, half-dream, conjured not by the secret songs of snake charmers, but by heat and an abiding silence that frames his mother's face from memory: a black-and-white photograph. She's young, Mona-Lisa kneeling on the sand beach at Galveston, arms relaxed along her thighs; her one-piece black swimsuit creates deep shadows that seem to dissolve her arms and knees into a single moment of darkness. A busy sand beach stretches behind her, and beyond, hundreds of children thrash in rows of waves that crest white.

So many children, so far out.

In another photograph, her face is older, the mother of an only child, cheeks high but defined by time and worry; placid lines of her mouth are now an accusatory frown that no one should have taken her picture. She stands before her clothesline in far-north Canada, Marten River, where she's waited all day for her son and husband to return with the day's catch—some lake perch and one toothy pike. She's obviously cold, wears a thick sheepskin-lined coat, and a kind of mad bomber's hat. At her feet is a black cast iron frying pan with a glacial chunk of congealed bacon grease leftover from what her husband called their "wilderness breakfast."

In a little while, a thin veil of clouds half-covers the sky like a gauze shroud rolling out from the west over the Baltic Sea. Snakes above the great dunes vanish.

His mother's two faces are the only faces he remembers.

* * *

IT'S LIKE HER to never leave out *anything*.

She says: Now that he's supposed to be grown up, if I even try to get within a hundred miles of him, kilometers, whatever, he gets nervous and acts like he has all kinds of big-shot things to do.

I ask him on the telephone, Are you staying away from milk, cheese, stuff like that?

But he says, So what if I'm not?

So I say, You're crazy, and get real mad at him, but then I calm down because I remember right after his father died, I caught him in the bathroom standing at the mirror, holding a Boy Scout knife to his throat.

I said, What in God's name are you doing?

What do you care? he replied, shutting the door and leaning against it with his smart-ass lean, but he doesn't know how strong I am, especially when I bring my elbows in, knees together, and lunge with my forearms. I pushed as hard as I could—I asked God to help me—and the door flew open and I took that knife from him and stuck it even tighter against his throat.

You want to die? I screamed. You try those shenanigans again and I'll kill you myself!

* * *

A LITTLE SOMETHING for the eel-woman.

Three kiosks over, he stops and buys two yellow mums, wrapped in yesterday's news, *Lietuvos rytas*. He remembers that past March when the eel-woman taunted him: it was   International Women's Day and what did he have for her? Nothing, of course.

He pulls the newsprint over the tops of the mums and tucks them into the side pouch of his satchel.

When the line at the ungurys kiosk slows, he waves the eel-woman out; she blinks in the afternoon light under her mop-top hair, pencil brows. He presents the two mums to the eel-woman, hoping she'll remember his *faux pas* last March, a compensatory grin on his face.

Why do you give me funeral flowers? the eel-woman asks.

Then he remembers he's been warned that in Lithuania two flowers are a sign of death. For a moment, she fingers both little tufts of yellow, as if his gesture may overcome her mildly horrified, subtly confused expression.

Will you go for coffee with me sometime? he asks.

You don't know me, the eel-woman replies.

I do, he says, you are the eel-woman.

So *that's* what I am? she says sarcastically. Then you must know my mother, Mother of the Eels, who lives in a beautiful garden under the Marios. Do you?

She hands the two yellow mums back to him with a weak, pitying smile, or so it seems to him when he flees the kiosk for the marina.

* * *

IT'S JUST LIKE her to be last off the plane.

The steward goes to her seat.

Ma'am, it's time to deplane.

Deplane? That man has a gun!

She scoots forward in her seat and points out the window of the airliner, where a soldier stands by a bus with a rifle slung on his shoulder.

That gun is only a formality, the steward tells her.

Formality, she says, my foot.

Eventually, she moves, so slowly, ducking from time to time to peer through other passengers' windows to steal a glimpse of the solider with the rifle. With bold trepidation, she descends the exit stairs, in careful, fluid motions. Her gaze falls to her big toes; one stair step, two, three. People on the bus wait patiently until she boards it, and the college exchange student relinquishes his seat for her, stands and takes the pole, twice gallant in the same day.

Her carry-on bag is stowed by yet another man.

She gives the Lithuanian soldier a menacing, distrustful look.

Once through customs, she enters the lobby of the airport, where flowers seem to bloom above a crowd searching for family members. She feels suddenly ashamed, alone, yet wades into the field of flowers bobbing on a sea of shoulders.

She is only halfway to the exit when she is set upon by a school of Russian taxi drivers.

One driver says, Cheap New York City rates—only fifty U.S. to the Center!

He places his pudgy hand on her suitcase.

Fifty dollars, my foot! she says.

She wrenches her bag free of the man's hand, then thrusts her way to a far corner of the lobby, where she finds a driver willing to take ten dollars to transport her to the youth hostel: Tolimas, affordable, out of the way, but where she's certain to be conspicuous.

* * *

RETURN OF THE eel-woman.

But not before he eats half the ungurys and buys a third mum, white, one that seems to go nicely with the two yellow flowers. He finds a bench near the water, sits, holding the mums, sleepy in their newsprint. A little later, he removes the mums from his satchel, carefully peels the wax paper away from the three flowers, takes two yellow ones, tosses them at the wake of a tour boat as it breaks against the tires tied to the pilings, and watches as they are sucked under, vanishing.

He removes the white mum from the newsprint and turns it by its stem in his lap. Then he folds the skin-flap over the uneaten portion of the ungurys, rolls the newsprint around it, and puts it in his satchel.

When the eel woman arrives, he has pinched the stem of the white mum so hard the chlorophyll stains his fingers. She reaches to remove it from his hand, and he draws it to one side, away from her.

Now you don't want me to have it? she asks.

* * *

THE NEMUNAS.

A road pirate takes her to Kaunas, no transport license, cheap fare, one Mr. Karmūza who deposits her on the speedboat to Nida along the Nemunas River, telling her what a pleasure it is to meet the mother of an American writer. When the boat pushes away, and for most of the trip, she sits as far from the liquor bar as possible and crosses her arms over her chest. Most of the crew on the speedboat down glass after glass of konjakas, until they are loud and singing what they must think is eloquently. A stranger sits across from her and brings with him a large snifter of konjakas. He proudly sets the snifter on the table between them. She notices the small veins variegating the tissue high on the stranger's cheeks, for her a sure sign of the man's impending death.

Labas, she says to the stranger.

It's like her to have asked Karmūza to teach her to say, Hello, son, in Lithuanian: "Labas, sūnau," like her to break the "labas" from the "sūnau" just to get the stranger's attention.

Labas! she repeats and points to his snifter of konjakas, Labas—No! That's what killed my husband!

She points again, which now startles the stranger, who grins, obviously knows not a jot of English, picks up his snifter, and greedily sips the tea-brown drink in spite of her warnings. She places her hands about her throat, pantomimes choking herself, makes gagging sounds at the stranger, who turns away from her, to the window, which draws her attention to the Russian side of the Nemunas River, to Kalingrad, its dilapidated buildings and expressionless women with their wash and children atop rocks at the water's edge, watching the speedboat as it churns by.

When the engines throttle up, she is overcome by the spell of water piling under the steel hull of the boat, water shearing itself from its other half, which rolls out in a shallow wave to break on the riverbank. She is taken by sadness and the drone of the engines; it enters her body; she shivers and suddenly feels fearless of the stranger opposite her, fearless of the other people on the boat. She turns to the stranger and stares at him a long time until he turns back to look at her, to sip his konjakas, and she begins speaking aloud to no one in particular since no one on the boat understands what she says.

The stranger blinks once, and she begins:

I want you to know that, though you are allergic to my milk, I can come, mano sūnau. I can come all this way...

She says this straight into his vacant and faraway eyes.

He blinks again.

* * *

THERE'S A THRUM in the pan-gray surface of the Marios.

The speedboat.

Your mother, the eel-woman says, staring across the Marios. She is just past Rusnė now.

He tells the eel-woman he knows Rusnė. When he first came to Nida, he'd made it as far as Šilutė, so low on money he broke into the abandoned jail in town, the old KGB offices, to sleep. The next morning, he found a young driver to take him to Rusnė, where he could get a skiff across the Marios to Nida.

Where in Rusnė? the driver asked.

He was so tired he didn't know or care.

Just take me to the water, he said.

When the driver rolled up to the water's edge, he got out and stood face to face with a large black bull kicking huge divots of grass and mud into the air with such anger that the driver sped away and he ran waist-high into the Marios before the bull broke off its pursuit.

The eel-woman laughs, stops.

You want me to laugh at you and this bull, right?

Well, he replies, not exactly.

Alright, then here's a funny thing, she says. About the beautiful garden of the Mother of Eels under the Marios. It was so beautiful that none of her eel-children wanted to leave. It became so overrun that the Mother of Eels could not care for them all. So, at dusk, she sent them to creep out the Marios and feed on milk from the udders of willing cows.

Willing cows? he says. What makes you think they are willing?

The eel-woman presses her moist hand into his.

I don't know, she whispers. I will need to ask my eel-mother.

He hands her the pinched white mum.

His thoughts fly out to the unsettled surface of the Marios, the speedboat bearing down.

Here she comes, he says.

BURN BARREL

COLE SCRATCHED THE Ohio Blue Tip match on the striker, watched the sulfurous flame pop, fronds of fire erupting like a blazing weed suddenly come to life. He touched the match to the blue book he'd crumpled and free-thrown into his mother's kitchen sink, his final examination last semester before graduating from college, the question contained there, and his response, a metaphor for the Underground Man's "conscious inertia," a freight train fully loaded with thoughts, sitting, clouds of exhaust billowing out the engine, and no one to drive it out of the station. It was also a perfect metaphor for Cole, the English educator of tomorrow, jobless, stuck at Station Recession.

The blue book first burned like a black-centered violet, to Cole's thinking a black hole that swallowed job applications of all spectra. Then it puffed into a crimson carnation, expending its energy, obliterating the professor's red A, dying ash black. He reached into his mother's sink, where flames of the Underground Man faced pointless extinction, snagged the smoking blue book, and deposited it into a coffee can containing pencils labeled OTSEGO. The pencils sputtered into flame—one, four, nine—until the flames breached the rim of the can like hungry luminescent new teeth wanting more fuel, consuming the imprint OTSEGO, name of a county first called Okkuddo, a Native American word for stomach pains, soon changed by embarrassed legislators to the Iroquois name Otsego, derived somehow, as Cole understood, from "sago," a greeting meaning "I'm still alive" or "yet well," though the pencils bearing the name were now neither well nor alive, combusting in the coffee can.

Otsego was Cole's old high school, where his mother worked mornings, six to nine, caring for latchkey kids from the elementary school, then helping in the cafeteria. For a time, his mother's part-time job and the small death benefit from his father's life insurance would be enough. But not for long. Cole's metaphorical train didn't seem to be leaving the station for quite some time.

When the Otsego flames diminished, Cole found a dish rag, seized the hot coffee tin, and carried the fulminous vessel through the back door into the chilly Ohio fall air. He elbowed the lid of the charcoal grill aside, pulled out the grate, and spilled the sizzling kindling into the pot. He tossed in a few self-igniting briquettes, then went back inside, got his coat on, and returned to see heat shimmer in the air above the grill, the edges of the briquettes frosting white.

Cole waited, noticing the conspicuous silence of the birds, neighbors, traffic, and freight trains that usually rumbled by the small house several times a day carrying heaps of coal to the power plant in Toledo. When the briquettes glowed, he went back inside and returned with a stack of school things, and one-by-one dropped them into the belly of the grill; first, a letter informing him of his Dexter Scholarship for the Balanced Man, one his mother'd sent in without his knowledge, presented to incoming male students, most the ripe old age of eighteen, who had "led a virtuous, diligent, and balanced life, and having a sound body and mind." The scholarship was a thousand dollars out of the twenty-eight thousand it took him to get his degree and to get loans that needed to be repaid, shadowy amorphous creatures that now seemed to perpetually loom at the horizons of the Balanced Man.

Into the fire went the Balanced Man, along with class notes, examinations, instructions, diagrams, research papers, and an equal volume of bursar's bills, late payment, and eviction notices. Everything burned and balanced. Knowledge and its cost. But he could not afford to burn his books. They may be worth something, though he knew not much, except perhaps his chemistry text, *Getting Excited About Atoms*, the course he dreaded and put off until his penultimate semester, a text that ran him $279.95 plus tax, a good chunk of which he hoped to recoup since he'd bought the latest edition. Even The Book Pirate: No, Seriously would not deny him decent remuneration, despite the store's ridiculous attempt at ironic humor in its name.

Cole watched his school papers burn. He tried to think. To worry about his student loans. His future. A job. He tried, but he couldn't think. So long as the fire burned, and he stared into its hypnotic flames, he couldn't think a thing.

* * *

"WHEN I SAID keep the home fires burning," his mother said, "I didn't exactly mean this."

She reached into her sink, removed a handful of ashes, then rubbed them between her palms, like she was washing away the stink of cafeteria work after her stint with thirty-odd latchkey kids. She ran a little water over her hands and turned to face him. He was close, for he had a habit of following her about the house the first five minutes or so when she returned from anywhere, a habit he'd picked up in high school after his father died.

Back then, he'd trail her, asking questions about details of her day, people she met. Now, he stood behind her, silent, then said, "I took the fire outside."

She glanced out the back window where, above the grill, papery hot ashes rose, then drifted down onto a dusting of snow from a late October squall. She smile-yawned and quickly raised a fist to her mouth to cover both, with the slightest, "Ah-o-ah" escaping, then noticed the pencils and coffee tin missing from the sill in the kitchen.

"I suppose since you've graduated, you don't need anything to write with anymore?"

Then she smile-yawned again, the same gesture nearly every day after work. He could never tell if the smile covered her yawn or the yawn covered the smile, only that her fist covered both.

"I'm just burning old school papers," he said.

He followed her into the living room, where she dropped her purse on the sofa, her derrière nearly beating it there.

"Okay, just do it in the burn barrel out by the garden." She smile-yawned a third time. "I don't want the ghosts of your calculus problems haunting me when I'm grilling my burgers."

She rotated herself to lie on her back, ankles propped high on the armrest, the same fist she used to beat away her smile-yawn now at her forehead.

"How's the job hunt?" she said. "How was Monster.com?"

"Monstrous," he said. "Sent five more today. That makes fifty-two rejections."

"Hey, maybe fifty-three is the charmed number," she said.

"Whoever heard of fifty-three being charmed?" he asked.

But by then she was asleep.

He covered her with an afghan and suddenly the room became golden, an afternoon sun coming out clouds that lit up yellow curtains over his mother's sink, diffuse light streaming into corners, eliminating shadows, leaving his mother's face luminous.

In such light, he caught himself thinking again, what the big deal was with college things, no job. Watching his mother's chest fall and rise, he doubted he could ever leave home anyway. He told himself it wasn't time to make a change. Maybe she needed him. He couldn't be sure. Why would she? Did it matter? He just needed to relax. Nothing else. Just that. But it wasn't just that. He needed her. His education made him just smart enough to know he needed her. But it also taught him perhaps he ought to not need her. He was young. He should just leave. Not be a burden. Go anywhere. Do anything. But he'd miss her. Just that. How could he ever explain it to her? Just that? And so he didn't want to need anyone or anything as he wheeled the grill to the old burn barrel by the garden, rusted from a decade before when his father set it there and cold-chiseled air holes in the top half.

After he poured the coals into the barrel and hosed out the grill, he walked out to the road where the autumn cornstalks chaffed in a new wind rising from the southwest. In the north, trees lining the Maumee River were an odd mix of colors, on the whole, a dull mantel of browns and greens, splotched with eye-popping reds and yellows.

When Cole made it to the railroad crossing near their house, he followed the rails a couple dozen ties down, until he reached a shallow ditch choked with dried-gray thistle. There he found a few ends of throwaway ties left from when the company'd repaired the crossing last fall. The creosote was sticky on his fingers and he dreaded holding the pieces of ties close to his coat, but the trip back was short and so the ties didn't make much of a mess. He dropped the tie-ends by the burn barrel and went inside. A sponge, a little soap in the kitchen sink, a slow, quiet stream of hot water from the faucet to not wake his mother, and he was clean.

When he returned to the burn barrel, he dropped a tie-end inside. The burn barrel coughed black balls of smoke skyward. The creosote. By the time the belching flames licked the rusty rim of the barrel, he heard the doorbell ring inside the house, his mother rise, then an odd pause before she answered it. When he started inside to see who it was, he saw his mother head for him double-time with a raw hotdog on a skewer, the sheriff trotting behind, a big man with an abundant gut held by full county regalia, replete with stun gun, Beretta, and radio clicking and hissing.

"Here," she said to Cole, and handed him the skewer with the impaled hotdog.

The sheriff halted at the burn barrel, looked at the cold wiener and skewer in Cole's hand.

"I suppose he's having a little cookout," he said to Cole's mother.

"Yes, he is," his mother replied, then yawned, a huge, gaping, I'm-tired-officer yawn, sans smile, sans stifling fist.

"Well, I suppose you know the ordinance," the sheriff said to Cole.

"Yes, he does, sir," she replied, nudging Cole to direct the wiener into the black-tinged flames. "No open burning except for family cookouts. Well, he and I, we're a family. And this here's a cookout. Sir."

"Then the Finkles," the sheriff said, attempting to tug his gun belt over a particularly stubborn roll of belly fat, "must have made a mistake when they called us."

By then, Cole's wiener was black with creosote residue. The sheriff and his mother paused to watch the morsel shriveling.

"He likes them burned," his mother mumbled, then her voice rose to meet the skeptical look in the sheriff's eyes. "I mean, he likes them *really* burned, officer. Don't you?"

The sheriff walked off without another word, officiously shaking his head.

Just as the front door closed behind the sheriff, one of the ties popped in the barrel, and his mother spotted the other tie-pieces at his feet.

"You can't burn ties," she huffed. "They'll explode. If this is something you gotta do, take some from the woodpile."

Then she left, walking slowly back to her cozy couch, as if when she awoke, his business with the burn barrel would be done.

In went pine, apple, maple, black walnut, pieces from quarter- and half-cords, pieces so gray and bug-eaten he swore he remembered stacking them with his dead father years before.

* * *

HIS NEED TO get to The Book Pirate: No, Seriously was more than economic. Selling his books, ridding himself of all the years of thinking and planning was a kind of combustion itself, not a hot burning, not like Guy Montag's tragic 451-degree Fahrenheit flames, but flames of conscious forgetting, cold combustion, a breakdown of his past, and future, indifferent to the dreams he once held of teaching something to someone somewhere, to knowledge he now felt would die with him in old age, knowledge alone and forgotten, dying like the embers of who he thought he might become someday. So long as he fed the barrel, so long as he kept it burning, it would be there for him, its mesmerizing comfort, its seemingly eternal flames of unlearning, to burn away time and knowledge and despair.

He turned away from the burn barrel, went inside, and woke his mother on the couch.

She swiveled upright, wide-eyed.

"I'm going to sell my books," he told her. "You gotta keep the barrel going until I get back."

She seemed so relieved that he'd come out of the cold, he wasn't surprised when she said, "Sure," but was when she added, "What?"

He lied: "I want to have a nice burn tonight. It helps me think, you know, about the future and whatever."

Later, when he pulled up to The Book Pirate: No, Seriously, the owner, Mr. McCall, was out on the sidewalk, taking in the brisk fall day, easy to spot because his neck sank far down between his shoulders, as if he had an iron weight pressing squarely on his head. He seemed to be eyeing college students like they had personal dollar signs and figures floating above each.

Cole preceded McCall inside and set his books on the counter. On top was his pristine *Getting Excited About Atoms*.

McCall took each book, dutifully clicked in the ISBN 13s, while casually leafing through pages to check for damage.

His chin came up before his eyes met Cole's.

"I'll give you fifty dollars for all," McCall said.

"But *Getting Excited* cost me over 280 bucks!"

"New edition's out, kid. It's worth about $25 now."

Cole took the fifty, not in anger or capitulation, but in relief that he was simply and completely rid of something, the way a snake moves cleanly out of its old skin.

But the way home, somehow it got to him. Driving on Mitchell Road, where either side dry cornstalks rose high like two solid walls, he felt trapped. He could see forward and backward but didn't feel he had the choice to simply pull over and clear his head and rid himself of the damnable, impenetrable cornstalks, leaving him no choice but to move forward at a greater and greater speed to leave them behind.

He finally burst out of the terminus of the two cornfields, feeling free, then slowed, thinking about getting home and stoking his softly snapping fire.

When he entered the house, his mother was sleeping again, and he could see out the back door that she'd let the barrel go cold—no heat snakes, no combustion he could see to clear the pointless fog of knowledge that prepared him for—what? A career in fast food? A benefit-less, ass-kissing go-nowhere nothingness?

He pressed quickly through the back door, pulled it closed behind him, found a willow stick lying in the yard, and rushed to inspect the burn barrel for any sign of fire. He poked at the residue in the bottom with the stick and found one coal, one precious scrap of possibility. He looked around the yard for paper, kindling, anything to rescue his fire. Finally, he opened his wallet, spotted the picture he still carried of a Goth girl from high school—Bianca?—who broke up with him right after prom, and who'd inscribed his yearbook, "When you say you hate children, I think it's so sexy."

He slipped her photo from his wallet, bent over the rim of the barrel at his belt, no small feat, even for a "Balanced Man," touched the corner of the photo to the dying coal, and watched it ignite.

After that, everything went into the barrel, the site of his disintegrating existence, its blackened gullet. He tossed in high school photos, achievement certificates galore, coach awards, chess club tournament championships, Glee Optimist of the Year, National Honor Society scrolls, National Merit plaques, a couple other national things or other. In went yearbooks. And then he worked backwards to his middle and elementary years, way back to his first attempts at cursive, huge curling letters, atop the pages his teacher's fragile stars with adhesive paste dried and flaking, barely clinging to the paper, her big red GOOD! scrawled under each star. He went back to preschool, blue, yellow, red swirling finger-paintings, clouds of color behind which he had no memory. All went into the barrel to keep the blaze alive.

He was angry for once, angry at his mother for neglecting the fire, but also angry that he'd not seized the chance to burn things away before, angry at the missed opportunity, time wasted, angry that he'd not been angry enough before, enough to find the means to eliminate all knowledge, to see its true limits, to test its nature, its prophecies of employment and happiness, all in the light of simple combustion.

In his anger of missed opportunity, he found one last batch of things, his baby pictures, begging the very question of his existence, before memory, then realizing that this baby, his baby-self, seemed the most photographed baby on Earth: baby on pony, on train, on boats, with telephones, in the mouth of an amusement park whale, baby as sailor, doctor, fireman, so many occupations he'd had when an infant. How? Goddamn baby had plenty of careers. He couldn't get a thing now.

He raised both fistfuls of baby photos, ready to dash the last evidence of his existence into the burn barrel when he felt her take both his wrists.

"I don't care what you do with the rest of your fucking shit," his mother said. "But those photos are mine. Not yours!"

One hand each she extracted the baby photos from his fists, spat in the burn barrel, and marched back into the house.

He watched the flames in the barrel begin to die one by one.

Later, his mother rejoined him there, arms crossed, staring at the last wisps of smoke drifting past the rusty rim of the burn barrel.

"Does it really help to stare into that old barrel?" she said. "Don't you want to remember anything from those years?"

His mother was silent then, not in an expectant way, but in her way of waiting, and their silence left them looking to the north, toward Waterville, where they noticed another fibrous string of smoke rise high into the windless air. In the west, a thread of light from the setting sun caught two more columns of smoke with a pale orange luminescence. South, in the direction of Tontogany, a fourth column rose. Behind them, at the Smiths, a more determined smoke seemed to climb a rope into the sky, fist over fist. Soon, more vaporous pillars drifted upward from neighbors and villages around them, until night fell, and all that remained was the acrid scent of burning everywhere in the raw Ohio air. Everywhere, burning.

His mother shook her head.

"Come on, Cole," she said, "we better be getting inside."

HEATING AND COOLING PEOPLE

SUMMERS, MY IN-LAWS care for all the cooling equipment breakdowns that occur around the flat, hot village we live in. Winters, like this one, they respond to heating emergencies, with all the requisite equipment. A landline's attached to a dusty answering machine on a marble planter in the front room. On a desk nearby, two-part carbon form receipts sit, layered like baklava. The garage, two rooms over and down, is stocked with flexible conduit, pipe, pine boxes of fittings, and Lennox supplies. The interior of their home is emerald. A cold white light beats through thick, green, rubber-backed drapery. The house is warmed with a steady stream of air running in invisible sheets from the floor vents.

My father-in-law reads the paper in the La-Z-Boy chair in the front room. His feet are up. The TV mumbles, the dishwasher churns. My mother-in-law is in the kitchen, working through a stack of cold cuts with her fingers, sorting slices of pale meat onto white bread, asking me when Sharon and I will ever get together again. I tell her I think we're through for good this time. She tells me to give Sharon a little time, reminds me how Sharon's not like me. How she lets things build up and then she explodes; people are always catching the fragments and, even if I am her husband, I'm going to get some of the fallout.

"I'll never understand what's eating her," I say. I carry my sandwich to the table and sit opposite my mother-in-law. "She's your daughter."

I hear my father-in-law roll up from the La-Z-Boy. I lean a little left and look in on him. He sits stiff-spined, then stretches two fists in the air, and begins stacking sections of the newspaper on the footstool. He's a large, square man, wears T-shirts, corduroys, and white tube socks, says they're from his summer collection, summer insofar as they remind him of better days. He used to pitch for the Brooklyn Dodgers, came up from the farm team one season, and you can see it in his bones and tan complexion. He got in one good season, a three-point-seven ERA, won five out of nine games, then got hurt. But I had to get all that from my mother-in-law, since he doesn't talk about the glory days, only heating and cooling, and how the hospital probably owes him ten thousand bucks by now with all the charity work he does over there. He's quick to explain how, in winter, they can't go without heat for even a couple hours.

My mother-in-law says to him: "You don't get summers or winters off, buster. You know the Marine vet that lives the far end of Liberty Hi Road? He's been without heat two days now. You need to get out there."

"Okay," he calls into the kitchen. "But how about some lunch for *me*?"

She plants two hands on the arms of her chair, rises a little, and hangs like that a couple seconds, suspended in a squat above the seat, considering his request.

"You got a call, remember?" she says. She walks over to him and hands him her sandwich. "Here. Eat this in the truck."

I hear him get up, his boots pounding on the stairs leading to the basement. He works the side door open and goes into the garage. I hear the van start, then the groan of the engine dissipating in the distance down the street.

* * *

I KEEP IN touch with Sharon through my in-laws. She works one town over at Suzie's Hallmark by the Krogers, and my mother-in-law is over there so much I give her messages from the home front to take in to her. We haven't lived with our in-laws or anything like that. We rent an efficiency apartment, but her folks' place has whole-house air and humidified heat. Three bedrooms. One-and-a-half baths. It's nice here. Comfortable. "Civilized, right?" my mother-in-law has a habit of saying.

There were some good summers for Sharon and me, two or three leading up to the last one, which was when things got bad. Sharon tells me our marriage is just a piece of paper. I tell her maybe this month I'll find a job, maybe I can even help her dad out with the heating and cooling work. Who knows? Would that make our marriage any better? Maybe I could have my own business, I tell her. But that just makes her madder. I think Sharon hates the idea that I could make it like her old pop. Sometimes, I think she's serious about us separating for good. Then I think how absurd it is, how friendly things are at my in-laws. So, I go over to the in-laws a lot when Sharon and I are fighting. I wind down, knowing she'll come around when things get better.

Now I'm pondering the idea of asking her pop to be his apprentice, but I wonder if winter is the best time for it. Winters are the worst, very busy. And cold. She takes the calls, which ring in torrents throughout the day. He makes the calls: big jobs, small jobs, a lot of odd jobs. Heck, it's okay for him. It's pretty steady work, which is why I'm not so sure about it for myself. I really want to put my English degree to work, somehow.

"We've got six people with busted piping," she tells every caller today. She soothes one of them through the receiver: "You poor dear. A wheelchair? He can be by this afternoon."

He's out most of the day. Sometimes, he comes in between calls. He comes in from the last one, goes downstairs to the sink in the basement, and wrings his hands and arms with Lava soap like a surgeon in post-op.

"That house is full of gas," he hollers up the steps. "They want to stay there, though. I ran a temporary line for them. I think they're crazy if you ask me."

For a moment, she seems to ignore him, then says, "Well, mister, nobody asked you!"

He goes back out. Sharon calls and my mother-in-law gets it.

"What does she want?" I ask, while she goes on jawing with Sharon on the line, but the whole time, she's looking at me, wagging her head. "What *is* it?" I say.

My mother-in-law hangs up the phone. "Nothing," she says. She butts the refrigerator door closed with her hip and brings over some cold sauerkraut balls in a bowl. She sets the bowl on the table, pauses to see if I'm interested, then brushes the bowl my way with the side of her hand. She reaches in and hands me a ball.

"You keeping me company all day?"

"Sure."

"Then make yourself useful and eat these before they go bad."

* * *

WINTERS, MY MOTHER-IN-LAW brings out her gadgets and sets out her decorations. This year, she has an extraordinary inventory, since this is soon after Christmas, and she has added antiques to the old staples. She calls them her pretties and particulars. This winter, her particulars include three pre-Korean Conflict AM radios, an old Bearcat Police Ban Scanner, and a vintage Radarange microwave oven. To make room for these, her newer gas oven in the kitchen is packed with boxes of cereal, bags of stale bread heels, and crumpled, halfway-devoured bags of Fritos. She cooks, when she cooks, in the old white-enameled range in the basement.

I find the full bathroom upstairs, undo, and piss as I look at another particular antique she's commissioned for use this winter, a Miami Carey intercom, now a common device throughout the house. Suddenly, I hear his voice come through the large oval shadow behind the wood-grained plastic slats.

"Coming up."

I'm baffled for a response, but then she comes in on the little speaker just behind him. "Those people two streets back got a bum furnace. You should get back out."

There are many more pretties than particulars throughout the house now, mostly lamps and limited-edition figurines. I suppose that's a hell of a generalization, perhaps insulting to the Hummels, little German kids poised in Bavarian bliss. Or the Rockwells, barefoot kids, dime-store people, and octogenarian dentists. She only puts out the tiniest 3-D scenes since, perhaps, the painter or designer can never quite duplicate a crease in the pants, the precise lay of a lock of hair. She likes them unique. Just like the lamps. They are all brushed brass and frosted glass or lathed-and-stained maple or oak. The shades and bases of the lamps are hand-painted with log cabins, broad-leaved trees, and Boonesborough-types leaning on squirrel rifles. The brush strokes have been laid carefully. Only where the artist has raised the brush, just at the end of a stroke, unique wisps of paint trail up and away.

I zip up, looking at a new pretty of hers atop the toilet tank, an oval plaster impression of a shepherd boy with two trumpets. It's supposed to be an exact replica of a 600-or-so A.D. piece. Roman, I think. She got it in September in Chicago at the sales counter at the Vatican Exhibit. Funny thing about her. She's never seen a day of church, never gotten much past lamp-art before. We were outside the Century Theater when she said, hawk-eyeing a bulletin board, "Vatican Touring Just Three Cities!" That day on, she would not be satisfied until we got tickets, got on the Amtrak, and went to see the pretties of the Papacy at the Art Institute. Funny thing about the shepherd kid with two trumpets. He's not in the exhibition, at least he's not mentioned in the audio self-guided tour or the commemorative volume of the exhibit.

"This guy never made it out," she giggled. "Must be back at the Vatican in Rome." That supposition seemed to make her desire the shepherd boy all the more.

* * *

MY FATHER-IN-LAW CALLS in from the 7-Eleven, coming in on the speaker phone: "Those people two houses back set their furnace at ninety degrees for a month to keep their house at sixty-five. They bought two of those old Kero-sun heaters on eBay. Ran them all the time. Jesus, they never went downstairs to check the furnace. The storm door down there was whopping wide open. It froze up everything. So I shut it."

My mother-in-law says into the speaker: "You need to see Mrs. Crowley. She's in that wheelchair. She doesn't have anyone."

"O-kay," his voice cuts in and out of the intercom sharply.

Sharon calls. She and her mother talk a little while. Usually, they don't talk about anything, only I'm wondering if I should be doing something while they're talking, like asking for the phone.

"What did she want?" I ask my mother-in-law when she hangs up.

"Nothing for you to worry about, dear," she smiles wryly. "She just wanted to know if you were here."

Later, while my mother-in-law and I microwave popcorn, I make a gross error. I tell her I'm trying to write a story about her Vatican Collection, with an angle on the collection as it might be seen through the eyes of a child: the innocent meets the inspired. I know she doesn't like that I started a Masters in English after marrying Sharon instead of getting a full-time job. She likes it even less when I mention writing. But now she shocks me. She's calling every rectory and the like in town.

"Oh, yes, my son-in-law needs to know where it says in the Bible, 'When I was a child I did childish things, then when I was a man I put them away'...Yes, yes, okay." Then she whispers with her hand over the receiver: ("I couldn't get him, but I got a nun.") "Yes, dear! One Corinthians. Chapter Thirteen. Verse Eleven. Uh-huh. Thank you, dear!"

I try to tell her the whole piece is dog shit anyway. She can't begin to know. I don't usually try non-fiction. In any case, she's ruined it sure with her damned research.

She grins, leaning over to light a votive candle in one of her brushed-brass lamps.

"See, I told you," she says and sets the phone on the hook. "New Testament, not Old."

I try to change the subject, tell her I've rented an orange Kia Rio for the holidays. The car is ten bucks a day from Rent-A-Duck. It's got a blue and yellow sticker on the back window: THE UGLY DUCKLING. She doesn't drive, and he takes the van to make calls. Since I have the car, she wants to go to the Hallmark to see Sharon. She says she and I should get out more together.

She slips on her rubbers and motions for me to follow her outside, where a new icy-wet snow has glazed over old powder, frozen, and shimmers in streetlamp light. She crack-crunches through the surface, making her way to the Ugly Duckling.

"It's awfully clean for an '05," she says, getting in, crimping her body over, inspecting the dash.

"I hate this duck," I tell her.

"Aw come on, there's no other duck like it."

Soon, new snow comes down in fat flakes. The duck grunts through it.

"There's Suzie's." She points. "Nobody's gonna be there now. It's dead time."

"When we go in," I say, "tell Sharon I'm sorry."

"Sorry for what?"

"I don't know. Just tell her I talked to you about how much I hate fighting with her—and make it sound like I didn't ask you to say anything, okay? Tell her we were just shooting the breeze and I happened to tell you I was sorry. You know what I mean?"

Little bells jingle in the doorjamb as we go into Suzie's. I feel like pissing again. The half-off Christmas stuff is up front. My mother-in-law says she's after tree ornaments. Suzie's are scattered on a tiered glass case. Not too badly picked over. My mother-in-law snatches eight of them, hangs them by limp threads in her fingers, and holds them close to her face. The ornaments dangle from her hands, clacking against themselves.

"Sharon's not here," I say.

"Maybe she's on break," she says, still adoring the ornaments. "Go ask the woman at the counter." When it's dead time, things are on sale. She seems to be in Heaven. "I always like to get just a little something each year after Christmas—and it's all so cheap!"

"You ask the woman at the counter where Sharon is," I whisper, getting sick at the thought that Sharon may have lied to me about working tonight.

The baubles continue to clatter, hanging from my mother-in-law's fingers.

"These are precious!" she says warmly, looking lovingly through the menagerie of wooden elves, rocking horses, reindeer, camels-and-kings. Suddenly, she snaps up a plain, thumb-sized ceramic angel that holds a crucifix. She drops the ornaments and finds another tiny angel, this one clutching a crown of thorns. She rummages awhile longer and comes up with a third angel carrying a long, sharp spear.

"These are the *most* precious!"

"Where do you think Sharon is?" I ask her. "Do you really think she's on break?"

She takes up the three precious angels, unsnaps her pocketbook, pays for them, and we go out to the car.

"Don't know what these are, do you?" she says to me several times on the way back to the house. She rolls the little angels around in her hands. "They're special." She holds one close to her face and reads a little tag stuck to one angel's feet. "They're 'Angels of the Passion!' That's really something, huh?"

* * *

WE'RE HOME, AND my mother-in-law is cooking pigs-in-a-blanket downstairs in the old gas oven. My father-in-law comes in with a loaf of bread under each arm. He's wind burnt.

"Oh my, those pigs smell good," he says to me and smiles, drawing his face into wrinkles. "Your mother-in-law here, she don't work." He catches his breath, hands her the loaves, cups his hands over his mouth, and blows into them long and steady. "She's a lover, not a worker."

"Shut up, you," she tells him, pulling the foil away from one of the loaves and retrieving a knife.

"After I worked over at Mrs. Crowley's," he says, "I went to the Rectory and unplugged their pilot. They gave me some of that priest bread, like every time I get over there. It'll go good with those pigs."

She cuts us all a piece of priest bread and we eat it. The bread is poppy-seeded, dry, but light and sugary. She sets her piece down half-eaten, goes into her Suzie's bag and comes out with an Angel of the Passion clutching the crown of thorns.

"We went by the Hallmark in his Ugly Duckling and got some pretties," she tells my father-in-law.

He takes the precious angel in his huge calloused hand and rolls it between his thumb and forefinger.

"Oh my…" His voice is distant. "You know, I was over to that House of Genesis, the one for battered wives, remember? I had to fix a leak, so I tried to call the gas company to send a man out to pull the meter so I could get to the leak. Wouldn't you know it, those women would not let me call? One of them says: 'We had to have you out here, but we don't want no one else.'"

"Come on, guess what it is!" my mother-in-law pleads, still intent on the angel pinched between his fingers. "Isn't it nice?"

There's a long silence. Then he says: "It's pretty, right?" and his words go off again, like he's not really with us. "You know that Mrs. Crowley?" he says. "She's that woman who acts so hard and mean from her wheelchair? You should've seen these big old tears come down her face when I got her heat back."

"Come on!" she says.

He inspects the little tag at the angel's feet, mumbling, "Angel of the Passion."

"Not only that," my mother-in-law says. "Here, let me show you." She pulls another Angel of Passion from the sack, goes over to one of her brushed brass candle lamps, pulls off the chimney, and jams the tiny angel, bottom-first, onto the flame. The hot wax oozes and curls around the bottom of the angel's tiny white smock.

"It's also a candle snuffer!" she exalts.

He glances at me strangely, with a tired face that may know more than a heating and cooling man needs to know. He hands me the precious angel and goes downstairs to wash-up and check the pigs.

Sharon calls in again. My mother-in-law snags the phone. She cups her hand over

the receiver. "Are you here?" she asks me. Then she is listening a moment into the earpiece.

"Who wants to know?" I say.

"Sharon," she laughs, moving her fingers over the receiver. Then she removes her hand altogether. "Yes, he's here," she says.

* * *

WE EAT LATE, and the pigs make me sleepy. I don't think about how they make me sleepy; they just do. My father-in-law and I are in the living room. He's in the La-

Z-Boy and I move into the rocker beside him. We have been cutting in and out of sleep all evening. Sometimes, I'm gone, and I suspect he is awake, hoping I'll raise an eyelid; then I'm up and he's gone, catching Zs.

I'm really drowsy, and I'm thinking: If we last the year, I'm thinking of taking Sharon to Bermuda. We can drive to Key West. Or fly. Maybe then we can get a cheap hopper to the Islands. Anyway, they're just sleepy thoughts. If I can remember them, I'll run them by Sharon when she's in a good mood.

When my father-in-law's dozing again, I go to the kitchen table, have another piece of priest bread.

When Sharon comes in, it's so late I can't remember her name.

"Oh, it's you," I mumble.

Then I wonder where Sharon's been. Unfaithful? No. Not around Christmas. Maybe she's been shopping, relishing it like her ma, only she wouldn't be doing it at Suzie's because it's not like her to be shopping in the same place she works. That would take the romance out of it.

Sharon comes over to the table, dragging her coat off her shoulders. She says she's tired. She just wants to go to bed. She sits by me and leans in close.

"I want you to go home," she whisper-hisses. "I don't want you here. I don't want you here anymore."

I try to tell her *The Late Show*'s coming on, the very next thing.

"Honey," I say, "can't I stay just a little longer? Maybe your old pa will tell us about his glory days with the Dodgers."

My mother-in-law comes in from the bedroom, goes over to the answering machine, and puts it on. She curls up on the floor at the foot of the television. My father-in-law's awake again. He crosses his white-socked feet over the top of the footstool. He shows me an exercise machine in one catalog, then picks up a new summer catalog, fans pages, and stops at dock-wear: light denims, breezy pantaloons, bright cotton shirts, and canvas deck shoes. He doesn't say a word. He just smiles. I smile. Then we are dozing again, together, and I am dreaming something I know I'll never remember.

DARNEL'S GARDEN

I have had a most rare vision. I have had a dream—past
the wit of man to say what dream it was.
                              —Bottom, *A Midsummer Night's Dream*

WALTER DARNEL WALKED the circular red brick
path through his mother's garden. Behind him rose a high
wall of old brick with a small iron gate in it that separated
the garden from a cliff, whose underside was scalloped
whole by the Pacific Ocean. He had returned from visiting
his mother at a rest home a few miles south of Santa Cruz,
during which time his mother, in her white cotton day
robe, and waving two stalks of limp asparagus at him,
asked him to search her garden for a sprig of sweet
marjoram.

"I doubt I will be able to find it," he said. "I'll try."

She handed him one stalk of asparagus.

"Well, then, there's rue for you, and here's some for
me," she said politely. "We may call it herb of grace 'a
Sundays." Darnel started to respond, but she interjected,
"Ah, ah, ah, mum's the word!"

Darnel reached into his breast pocket, withdrew his bifocals, and put them on. He passed a clump of herb plants inside the area circumscribed by the walk. Many of the plants had gone to seed, and he stooped to inspect the tiny yellow tags on each. A bunch of Lady's Mantle stood at the center of the weedy clump, its leaves like a Medieval cloak. He read the back of the tag: *Alchemilla vulgaris*. Below the seeding sprays, he noticed tiny hairs along the stalks and the undersides of petals, covered with droplets of dew, not yet burned away by the late morning sun. The light behind him slanted over the wall, caught the small beads of water, and colored the hoarfrost. He found another tag for a fragrant dropwort plant, one he knew had been a favorite of Elizabeth I for deodorizing rooms. He found other tags, some whose writing was nearly obliterated by exposure to the Sun. Others, he popped through thin crusts of soil at the base of a huge mass of intertwined plants.

He adjusted his bifocals and began to identify the plants: lemony coriander, anise-like chervil, dill, rosemary, sweet basil, English and French lavender, summer savory, three kinds of thyme—lemon, garden, and wild thyme— the pleated pods of finocchio, shallot, purple basil, costmary, the beery scent of alecost, horehound, lemon balm, sweet woodruff, and bitter pennyroyal.

The perimeter of the circular path was lined with the trumpets of white and gold lilies and daffodils. Although the daffodils had been planted in the front ranks of the tall stalky lilies, they also intruded in the lilies themselves, leaving discontinuous segments of lilies of all lengths. Honeysuckle had overtaken both the lilies and the daffodils, and climbed between, through, and over the tubers. The garden was fragrant with honeysuckle, and the papery white flowers seemed to veil and subdue even the brightest hues of the lilies and daffodils, the darkest greens of their reedy stems, leaving Darnel with the impression that they were covered with bits of confetti.

The corners of large, wooden planting boxes showed at the bases of the honeysuckle, through which he could just see dots of pink and pale yellow, the gillyflowers (his mother's term, as she preferred it to "pinks") and the primrose. The boxes were placed at various random orientations to the circular walk, some tangential lengthwise, some along their widths, others at points between these two attitudes. Two boxes of primrose appeared to be overturned entirely. Another box of gillyflowers was tilted to one side and a cinder block set beneath it.

Daniel turned back to the area enclosed by the circular walk. He knelt by a clump of herb plants and inspected the tags a long while, but at last, he gave up looking for the sweet marjoram for his mother. He was slow rising from his kneeling position—his mother was past ninety, and he past sixty. He managed to arch his back, straighten himself, then walk to the wall of old brick facing the ocean. From there, he spotted several patches of gray showing through the heart of the central clump. He sighed heavily and walked back to the mass of herb plants and into it, thrusting his feet forward first, under the tightly interwoven runners, then bringing his knees forward. He listened with regret to the snapping of stems as he followed with his hips and torso. At last, he faced a large mass of English ivy, shaped like a large bell. He took several vines at the top of the mass in his hands and pulled them apart. He noticed the outline of a short Doric column, then a flat round piece laid on top of it. He ran his fingers over the surface of the flat piece and detected the features of raised Roman numerals. He reached in, finally, and thrust his forearm to the very center of the clump, seized a woody vine that ran across the top of the flat piece, and drew it toward him. He shoved his other arm between the parted vines and felt another piece shaped like the jib and mainsail of a schooner.

He now surmised that he had found his mother's sundial and reached back to clear away more of the vines. When he saw the entire sundial, it was obvious that the gnomon was at one time fashioned in the shape of a single jib—but the curvate top portion of the gnomon had been damaged, a jagged notch in the jib the result. He cleared a few more wiry vines from the column and base of the dial, stretching them out and piling them to each side. He then freed himself from the vines and clump of herbs to find his mother's cropping shears. He returned and cut the vines and tops of several seed sprays nearby until the gray face of the dial showed in the morning light. The jagged gnomon cast two larger shadows, one about ten o'clock, the other about one. The actual time was lost—and lost him in thought. He heard the muffled sound of the surf behind him, beating. As a child, he'd played on the beach far below his mother's garden, in a tidal pool formed by dark, algae-bearded rocks. At sides of the rocks grew the green fleshy fronds of samphire—glasswort—the clusters of tear-shaped flowers in the centers of the plants.

He watched the two times on the face of the dial for some time, at once young and old. He recalled a beam of light he saw as a youth jutting from between two high, piled clouds, reaching over the gray wood of a half-buried boat at Half-Moon Bay. His mind was young; it was like some other old man occupied his life. It was the year growing old, not him. It was only the death of summer, the birth of trembling winter. He, on the other hand, would remain that prick of red that remained in the palest of gillyflowers.

Then his head emptied of everything except one thought: his mother's mind had given out before his, and perhaps his body before hers. The only matter, he mused, was which of them would wholly go first. But this all seemed too sad for him to continue to contemplate, especially here in his mother's stubborn and intransigent garden that was so like her. But the sadness he felt was more than the recollection of her intransigence, at which she was so graceful in her twilight years. It was a sadness of time, an essential sadness in the idea that his mother and he had grown so old, together, like three kinds of thyme—and time—in the garden, easy homophones: the fragrant, youthful scent of lemon thyme, the still point of garden thyme, and now, spreading and overrunning the garden, marching on and on and over his golden years—wild thyme.

* * *

HIS MOTHER'S GARDEN had not been cared for in five seasons, five seasons since Mrs. Darnel began, quite understandably, to neglect it. Before that, the garden was much more than Mrs. Darnel's garden. It drew the attention of the Shakespeare Society of Santa Cruz, whose president was Ms. Ruth Gennette, a hair stylist. The Board of Trustees was comprised of Mr. Wilson Charles, a bank vice-president with Security Pacific; Dr. Michael Minton, a geneticist; Mr. Otto Orgovan, a minor poet of growing reputation; and Dr. Jane Smith-Smyth, a corresponding member and Professor of English at the Orange County Community College. Mrs. Darnel had never joined the Society. She started and kept the garden out of private interest in Shakespeare, and frequently consulted with one Mr. Rasselas of the Rasselas Greenhouse about its care and upkeep. She gradually opened the garden to the

Shakespeare Society of Santa Cruz for various social functions and dramatic readings.

Darnel phoned Mr. Rasselas to see if he might locate a sweet marjoram plant for the elder Mrs. Darnel.

"I'm sure I won't have any sweet marjoram," Mr. Rasselas replied. "Say—" His voice rose an octave. "You going to do anything with your mother's garden?"

"I'm not sure," Darnel told him. "I'm not sure where to begin."

Rasselas made Darnel promise to call him if he needed any help with the garden, then added he'd try to locate the sweet marjoram at a supplier in Sausalito.

Darnel was surprised when Rasselas showed up an hour later at his doorstep. He was a tall man with thick eyebrows that grew together across the bridge of his nose. His skin was pale, slightly greenish. He wore a khaki jumpsuit with a white tag embroidered on the breast. The tag read RASSELAS in bright red thread.

"You know, I haven't been over here for years," he said. "I was just now driving home from work, and I was curious about what you might be doing with the garden. You mind if I have a look?" Rasselas went directly to the back patio door and out to the garden. "You may not be looking for advice," he said with his hands on his hips, "but I'd clear that honeysuckle right away and move those planters of pinks and primrose so the morning light can get at them. See—over there—about eight o'clock on the brick walk? That's where you ought to set them. Dig out the rest of the honeysuckle there or they'll be crawling all over them, then you can run rows of the lilies however you please. They don't mind the shade. Of course, these herbs, they'll take as much light as you'll give them. They're good right there at the heart of things."

Rasselas walked to the far end of the garden and stood at the twelve o'clock position on the circular brick walk. He pushed his way through the honeysuckle, then turned to face Darnel, who struggled to keep up with the determined gardener. Rasselas stripped several honeysuckle runners from an area to his right and presented Darnel with the bronze, heavily oxidized bust of a thin balding man with a sharply pointed beard.

"Here he is—Mr. Shakespeare."

The bust was a very thin version of the Bard, and one that endowed him with tufts of well-defined curls about the ears. It looked rather like Abraham Lincoln, not the other cherubic, limp-haired renderings Darnel remembered.

After Rasselas left, with one more promise to locate the sweet marjoram, Darnel decided that the best he might do for his poor vexed mother was to somehow unvex her garden. He cleared the honeysuckle away from a large planter of gillyflowers. He used a spade to loosen the soil around the base of one planter, then found a rusted grappling hook in the garage, looped a piece of nylon rope through its rusty eye, and set the hook in one corner of the planter. He heaved on the rope until the box broke free of the soil at its base, and gradually, grudgingly, scraped along behind him on the circular walk.

He was exhausted after moving the box onto the brick walk and surprised to find the light of day dying. He leaned on the bust of Shakespeare and watched the sky beyond the old brick wall and over the Pacific turn lavender, then blue-gray, then a deep purple. He slept deeply that night, remembering in a dream his wife, Charlotte, dead five years. She had left him five years before that to "do something, anything" with her life, "just one thing well." Darnel now felt, as his life grew ancient, that he too should do one thing well with his time remaining, something of consequence. He was not a fool, and he knew that good things, like bad ones, were transient. Too often, people themselves wore things away to nothing. His wife and he had produced a son, Edgar— but Edgar was anything but that moment of brilliance. He wanted in some way to produce a moment of brilliance, like the prick of red in the pale gillyflower.

It took Darnel a full week to drag the six planters from their spots under the honeysuckle onto the brick walk. By Saturday, he reached a point of physical exhaustion. He sat on the patio with his feet in a tub of cold water, a damp towel draped over his legs. His head was cocked back, and he was conscious of his breathing. For a time, this physical depletion, the cool morning air, and his deep, regular breathing cleared his mind. He seemed for the first time in a long while to understand his body, its limits, its finite nature, and the gift of the moment in which the agile mind can fully feel and comprehend the vulnerability of the body.

The doorbell rang and broke his meditation. He let the bell ring awhile in bursts of three, followed by the sound of knuckles tapping glass. When he was sure he would not be able to restore his former state of mind, he went to the door and answered it.

A small woman, wearing red, spiked heels, black pantyhose, and a tight blue dress stretched over her square hips stood in the doorway. Her hair was an odd shade of black, if not blue, Darnel thought, a kind of blue seemingly deeper in its dark appearance than black. It shone at its wiry edges like gun blue. She introduced herself as Ruth Gennette and offered her hand, which Darnel gladly, yet feebly, took.

"Mr. Rasselas told me you were resurrecting Shakespeare's garden. Walter, is it? May I have a look?"

Darnel led her through the house onto the patio, and to the garden walk. As he walked with her, he apologized for the garden's appearance, and he explained Mr. Rasselas's plan to allow the natural morning light to fall at about eight o'clock on the primrose and gillyflowers.

"Naturally," she said in a distant voice, "but I thought you might, of course, begin with the lilies at six o'clock, the spot at which an observer would first encounter them, and hence an allusion to one of his early histories." Darnel marveled at her use of the familiar possessive pronoun "his" in her reference to the playwright, and she continued. "I'm referring to *King John*: 'Therefore, to be possess'd with double pomp, to guard a title that was rich before, to gild refined gold, to paint the lily.' You see, Mr. Darnel, we might stand a plaque here at six o'clock or, say, sevenish, with that very quote inscribed on it. Then, of course, we could move straight-on chronologically, say, nine o'clock with the primrose and stand a plaque with something from a comedy—"

Darnel noticed that Ms. Gennette had become very animated. Her hands swept round and round like the blades of a great windmill when she mentioned the burgeoning of this or that planter or species, and she paused only to explain where which planter might best be placed to fit into her Shakespearean chronology.

"Yes, I think a comedy, say, *A Midsummer Night's Dream*: 'And in the wood, where often you and I upon faint primrose were wont to lie, emptying our bosoms of the conversal sweet.' Or, if you like, the pinks, 'the fairest flowers o' th' season...our streak'd gillyvors.' Certainly, the tragedy is all-around suited the center of the garden, your mother's exquisite herbs. But I rather think that the positions from twelve to six—the whole sweep, the day's half—ought to be a romance, don't you think? Let's say, *The Winter's Tale*: 'When daffodils begin to peer, with heigh! the doxy over the dale…' Well, there you are, Mr. Darnel. First the histories—the lilies—beginning here at sixish. Then moving on clockwise to the comedies—the primrose and pinks. Followed by the romances—the daffodils. And in the center, herbs for the tragedies—Rue, Rue, *Hamlet*—or is that overused? We shall have to see about that!"

Ms. Gennette then excused herself, offering to begin a complete concordance of allusions to flowers and herbs for Darnel's use. After she left, Darnel tried several times to reposition himself on the patio in such a way that might help clear his mind and rest his tired body. But each time, he could not block out the sound of the breakers beyond the wall, now amplified by the rising tide, or the memory of Ms. Gennette's unsettling, whirlwind visit. So he sat for a time, rubbing his legs until the doorbell rang again.

Mr. Charles, the banker, and Dr. Minton, the geneticist, arrived to tell him that they had also heard of his work with the garden, and they suggested two possible approaches to restoring it. Mr. Charles suggested that Darnel weed out the weaker species, and that he collect and cultivate only those that would most likely thrive in the garden. He offered to prepare a list of those Shakespearean plants which also seemed most well-adapted to the coastal climes of Santa Cruz. Dr. Minton, on the other hand, suggested that Darnel might tear out the herb plants in the center of the garden, and replace them with a kind of genetic code—a mixture, a pattern, a blueprint—of every plant he intended to propagate on the outer rim of the garden. This, then, would serve as a key to the larger pattern in the entire garden.

After Mr. Charles and Dr. Minton left with promises to submit their plans in writing for his consideration, Darnel once more returned to the patio, sat, rubbed his knees, and stared sadly at the six planters he'd pulled from the smothering runners of the honeysuckle.

Near dusk, Mr. Orgovan, the poet, stopped at the Darnel house. Still a bit confused, but in an exhausted state of good humor, Darnel asked Mr. Orgovan if he would like to see the garden. Darnel was indeed puzzled when Mr. Orgovan refused.

"I'm just here to say that you have no right to call it Shakespeare's garden. You can't possibly know the author's intentions for such a garden. I'm here to say, I guess, well—forget the whole thing. Why trouble yourself?"

* * *

DARNEL MADE SEVERAL starts in the garden, but he grew weary quickly. He stood at the ten o'clock station of the garden walk, and walked slowly, counterclockwise, pausing to stare at the garden from different hours of the clock, to see if a pattern emerged. He continued this for a long time until his eyes and head ached. He grew moody. He tried to get through *King John* several times as well, but failed after the first three scenes of Act I. The doorbell rang three times on three different days, and he refused to answer it. He thought of himself as a wastrel, a clod. How was he so different from a bit of clay, of red and brown matter, for the creeping clinging roots of others to push through?—around?—a bit of clay washed away and floating in the sea. He felt not at all like Donne's piece of the continent. Times like this, he felt like nothing entire in itself, no matter how low, fractional, or elemental. He simply felt pushed through.

Later that week, the sweet marjoram arrived, and Darnel drove out to Rasselas's Greenhouse to pick it up. The way back, he visited his mother. He often derived a great measure of joy at her physical stamina.

He asked her, "How would you like the garden? What shall I do with it?"

She reached out and placed her thin fingers on both sides of his face. Her face was bright, as if lit from behind. She spoke softly, and with a lucidity that startled him. "Sleep thou and I will wind thee in my arms...So doth the woodbine the sweet honeysuckle gently entwist; the female ivy so enrings the barky fingers of the elm. O, how I love thee! How I dote on thee!"

He handed her a sprig of sweet marjoram, kissed her forehead, and left.

The remaining drive home, Darnel made up his mind to sort through the various plans presented by Mr. Rasselas and other members of the Shakespeare Society of Santa Cruz. His thoughts began to poke and stab at the problem, but he drew a blank. The coast road was treacherous, even with his bifocals, so he concentrated on his driving.

When he arrived, he gathered his mail and walked to the patio. He found a letter from Professor Smith-Smyth.

Dear Mr. Darnel:

Mr. Orgovan has written to me and described your problem. Although Mr. Orgovan can, I fear, be rather gloomy about your prospects for a garden claiming to be "Shakespeare's," it seems to me that he is correct in his assumption that the claim of your garden to be the author's is absurd. But one cannot deny the existence of the garden! So let me hold forth some hope: I would suggest that you begin with one flower, or plant, and locate each in such a way that each additional flower highlights the difference between them—in fact, between plants, groups of plants, or whole sections of flora. Do not worry about an essential pattern; the placement of the plants, as they resonate with their direct allusions in the texts of Shakespeare, will be a tissue of contradictions, such as in *The Marriage of Heaven and Hell*. Even something as simple as a primrose may at once exhibit qualities of 'primrose' and 'not-primrose.' Given such a tissue of contradictions—differences—the pleasure a viewer might take in the garden might be stated thus: the essential apprehension of the pattern will be endlessly deferred; the garden will itself unveil a significant lack of unveiling— that the truth itself about Shakespeare and his plays is always hidden—happily.

Let me know if you have any questions or need further clarification.

Kind Regards,
Dr. Jane Smith-Smyth

Darnel set Smith-Smyth's letter aside. He removed his bifocals, set them on a table, and yawned. The great ache in his legs peaked, and he wondered if the pain would ever subside. Darkness was coming on. He began to turn all the proposals for the garden over in his mind, one after another. He searched for some happy middle ground or some thread that bound them all together. He walked the circular path through shadows and unfocused shapes that overran the garden. In the dusk, he marveled at how the garden looked so non-existent, so unreal, so "not-garden," he mused, applying Dr. Smith-Smyth's rule. How could he give each plant the light it deserved, allow for the heartier species, allude to the generic differences in the plants and Shakespeare's plays, create a blueprint, clarify the nonexistence of the author, and provide a tissue of contradictions? What about his mother? Would he ever decipher her unflinching devotion to an old playwright's words? How did she want the garden? Who could ever say what she really meant by her interminable recitation of fragments of the plays? —love? Of course, she loved him. But what about the garden? *Sleep…and I will wind thee in my arms…Oh, how I love thee…*Could she have meant those words for *him*, the plays, or the garden?

He once again piled it all very high in his mind. He walked slowly along the circular path, holding it all there, knowing and thankful that his mind was still good. When he reached the brick wall at the far side of the garden, the sound of a breaker below suddenly poured through the gate—the tide was up. Although he was sure he had reached the very limit of his mind's capacity, he could, for the moment, hold it all just so—and work the problem of the garden. He felt he had something; the wave swelled, crashed, and rushed away; then it was gone; for a moment, he felt a light gust of air brush his arm; yet the puzzle did not yield, nor did its pieces run out of his mind; but he knew, at least for a moment, that he could keep it where he wanted it; he could hold it all there…He rubbed his eyes, then opened the iron gate in the brick wall, and walked through it.

* * *

WALTER DARNEL'S SON, Edgar, sat on the patio turning a dram of white wine in the bottom of his glass. His father's bifocals sat on the table beside him. He had been thinking the whole time about the old man and watching the tangled lattice of pink and yellow trumpets, pink and white papery flowers, and green herbs in the garden. What could have been going through the old man's mind? How would he ever know his father's final inclinations, desires, intentions? It was beyond him.

Edgar swallowed the wine, took up the old man's bifocals, and turned them over in his hands. One theory was that the old man went through the gate without his bifocals and fell from the cliff onto the beach. The tide took the body out to sea. Another possibility, of course, was suicide. But could his father have ever harbored such a darkness of mind?

For Edgar Darnel, it was no matter, ultimately. There were others more capable than he to draw the needed conclusions. Dick Graham, the detective at the station, had been kind enough to assure him that the old man simply went over the edge. The bifocals left on the table in the patio were evidence enough. Edgar accompanied the detective to the rest home to question Edgar's grandmother. They found her as spry as ever, sitting straight up in her bed.

When Edgar asked her if Walter had visited her recently, she whispered low and secretively, "Alack, 'tis he!

Why he was met even now as mad as the vex'd sea, singing aloud, crowned with rank femiter and furrow-weeds, with hardocks, hemlock, nettles, cuckoo-flow'rs." She paused, reached under her pillow, and withdrew the sprig of marjoram. "Here's rue for you," she said and handed it to Edgar.

The detective asked Edgar if the old woman's words might be a clue to his father's disappearance.

"No," Edgar said. "It's Shakespeare."

After a time, Edgar decided that these matters—the particulars of his father's disappearance—were best forgotten for the sake of his father's memory. The garden was oiled and burned. The planters of gillyflowers and primrose strewn about the brick walk were burned in place. At the urging of Ms. Gennette, Edgar was fined five-hundred dollars by the Santa Cruz City Council for open burning. The bust of Shakespeare and the brick walk were acid washed. The soil was turned, and white mums planted in thick, perfect rows throughout the garden. The gate in the wall leading to the ocean was padlocked, and the broken sundial at the center of the garden that told two times was replaced with a bird bath, where most mornings, against the sound of the breakers exhausting themselves on the rocks below, two blue birds bickered well into the afternoons.

THE SADDEST STORY HE EVER TELLS

WHEN HE PULLED up that Friday night in December, I met him at the main entrance of my building, Winton Place, a high-rise condo overlooking Lake Erie. He had been an older student in my Thursday night Interpersonal Communication course, had a day job somewhere around Public Square, and asked me out just after the final examination. I laughed when he begged me to not "disconfirm" him.

He added, "I tell a mean story."

"By mean," I said, "do you mean a good story or an unkind one?"

I wasn't impressed—but I was so taken by his small hands nervously petting his maroon necktie that I surrendered my phone number without replying. His hands were lovely, almost divine, childlike, the way you see baby Christ's hands clutching his mother's neck in Renaissance paintings.

I slid beside him in his Soul, the car mice drive-in ads, one perfectly sized for mice, so small the faux fox collar of my coat touched his ear. The whole ten seconds in transit across the parking lot to Pier W, he kept brushing faux hairs away from his ear canal, worth the price of the cramped car ride since it afforded me a chance to look closely at his lovely hands, his slim fingers, pink, oval fingernails, cuticles like small white moons, nail ends slivers of opalescence, expertly filed.

I wondered why he'd chosen Pier W, a restaurant only a minute's walk across the parking lot from Winton Place. I supposed it was easy enough for him to google me, my condo. I'd gotten the down payment for it with help from my parents. They understood when I told them I needed a place on a high floor, twenty-six stories up. I had this fear of looking up, like vertigo in reverse. I needed to look down, though so high above things, and alone. I felt a little like Rapunzel without the witch Dame Gothel for company. After a while, the condo was a source of amusement for my mother. She'd call me "Zel" and I called her "Dame." I felt the words made us closer. I was an only child, and it'd been difficult for us both when I moved away from home.

"We're here," I laughed, expecting him to be surprised by the absurdly short ride, but he wasn't.

"Safe and sound," he said, like he knew all along where I lived in relation to the restaurant.

Pier W sat atop a raw concrete pedestal, the restaurant itself cantilevered high over Lake Erie, looking back on downtown Cleveland, building shaped like the head of

The Extra-Terrestrial in Spielberg's film. The Sun had set by the time we were seated. Out our window, I watched the city, its skyscrapers not nearly as threatening as walking downtown to my regular PR job at WJW–TV. The Key Tower, Terminal Tower, and Tower on Public Square each appeared like a mountain of light hovering in the dark, without foothills, floating above its own liquid reflection in the rippling lake water. My Zel-self wondered why Cleveland's tallest buildings came to be known as towers.

By the time the waiter brought the wine list, I was searching for an icebreaker, though my date appeared not to be. Only his hands showed, holding the list at his face; rude, I thought, but less so because of his fascinating hands, though after a time I grew so annoyed I nearly asked him outright why his hands were so small. Was he an anomaly of aging, betrayed only by his hands, in fact so young he may not be old enough to drink wine? I studied my own hands, slender, fingers perhaps a little long, yet still larger than his. In the pinkie of my left hand, I'd developed a trigger finger. Mornings, when I tried to bend it, there was this little hitch I had to press through before I could curl my pinkie fully. Because of it, my left pinkie leaned out a little from other fingers, like a poorly executed live-long-and-prosper sign made by Mr. Spock. I dreaded my errant little digit, something I felt inherited from my mother, whose arthritic hands had begun to curl and look like lobster claws. I googled my willful finger one wine-spirited evening, high in my Rapunzel's nest, finding that a leaning pinkie meant one resented her mother, though I could not think why, until the web page, I suppose as web pages do, also said the owner of a leaning pinkie would not be aware of such maternal resentment. I poured another glass of wine to celebrate the epiphany.

Other than being tiny, my date's hands seemed perfect. I'd dated men with huge hands, stubby-fat-finger hands, hands with nails bitten down to nubs, hands seeming without knuckles, hands with large knotty knuckles. Each, I was certain, meant some infirmity, some defect of personality, each no second date, each a dead end. But his hands were different, so small and surreal they seemed to exaggerate everything around them. Our white starched tablecloth seemed an expanse of the Arctic, his drinking glass not a goblet but a lapis-blue vat, silverware resting each side of his plate gleaming shovels and pitchforks. City lights through our window seemed to intensify each second he studied the wine list in silence. When I could no longer bear the Alice-in-Wonderland effect of all, I reluctantly spoke first.

"What's this mean story you mentioned telling?"

"Cabernet?" he asked.

"Fine—but about that story."

He set the wine list aside, and said, "How about a bottle of Poetry by Cliff Lede from the Stag's Leap District?"

I consulted my wine list.

"That's three-hundred dollars a bottle," I said.

"Oh, well, since you insist."

When the waiter arrived, he ordered instead the four-ninety-five-a-glass cabernet, Private Reserve, though I couldn't imagine how private or reserved it could be, since a majority of diners had glasses of it sitting at their tables.

We waited for the cheap wine.

"Oh," he said suddenly, "that story."

He leaned forward. His shirt cuffs drew up into his dark, cavernous coat sleeves, exposing his wrists.

So delicate.

"My mother."

I knew it. A story of the Jesus-baby's mother.

Our glasses of wine arrived. I smiled as he told me what a lovely woman his mother was. Short, with close-cropped carmine-colored hair. "Like wine," he said, taking the huge blue goblet lightly in the palm of one hand, swirling the cabernet, then setting it back without drinking.

I started to settle in for a long date. A man and his mother. I fought hard to not enter the disconfirmation zone. I looked back at the lake. I liked being high above the water. Then I noticed there were chains strung outside the large windows, festooned stanchion to stanchion, not looped high but low through iron eyelets, more decorative than anything, and I couldn't help wondering if the chains were to keep someone out, or in.

He said his mother was widowed. He lived with her in Toledo before coming to Cleveland.

My date brought the rim of the glass to his nose, like there was a point to ascertaining the bouquet of the Private Reserve, then lifted it to his lips and sipped—well, more like suckled—at the rim. He set the glass down, and settled back into his chair, his willow-thin wrists disappearing back into the caves of his coat sleeves.

I sipped my Private Reserve.

The waiter arrived at my elbow.

I said, "That's nice. I don't mean the wine; I mean your mother." I turned to the waiter. "Oh, the wine's nice, too."

He waited until the waiter left. Then he leaned forward, placing and exposing his hand and wrist on the tablecloth.

"That," he said, "was before my mother broke down and became schizophrenic. Before she shredded all my best suits, like the one I'm wearing, shouting, 'It's too damn dark in here all the time!' and took after me with a pair of shears."

I took a good pull on my wine, watched his hand dropping to his lap, out of sight. He settled back, as if he could sink so far he might melt into the chair.

Newly wrenched from the disconfirmation zone, I said, "That is a mean story. I mean, a sad story."

"But after a while," he added, "we got my mother help—meds and therapy at the Ruth Ide Center. Of course, after she attacked me, I moved out, got an apartment nearby, and checked in on her every so often."

Our waiter arrived again. I was glad to see him. I was a little rattled by my date's dinner conversation so far. I wanted the waiter to stay awhile, so I took my time, finally ordering the grilled Hawaiian bigeye tuna. I folded my menu and handed it to the waiter.

"I hope it truly has bigeyes," my date said.

"Oh, sir, it does!" the waiter said, wide-eyed himself.

"In that case…I'll have the walleye," my date said. He lifted his eyes from his menu to look at me. "Looks like the eyes have it tonight."

Corn. Usually a turnoff, if it had not been for the comic relief it presented in counterpoint to his mother's schizophrenia. I knew I was naïve about the world, but the shock of his disclosure about his mother didn't surprise me as much as his disclosing it to *me*. After all, I'd taught him in class about the limits of self-disclosure. Why would he make such a confession on a first date? Why would he follow with, "Speaking of my mother's needing more light, did you know the walleye has a special membrane behind its eyes to help it see in low light?"

Another moment of relief washed over me. He was simply *that* guy, the one who wanted to impress me with his encyclopedic knowledge. That guy I knew. That guy I could handle.

"It was at the Ruth Ide Center," he said, "that my mother met Truman."

It was then my date interlocked his tiny hands behind his head. I said nothing, annoyed that he'd secreted his hands away from me. I nodded. I smiled. I shifted in my seat. Sipped wine. Ran a hand through my hair. Tried everything to get him to unlock his hands and place them back on the table.

Finally, I said, "Well, go on."

He removed his Wonderland hands from behind his head, setting them on the Arctic expanse of tablecloth.

Truman, it turned out, was a man severely brain damaged when, due to heart failure, he hadn't breathed for twelve minutes. He was a resident at the Ruth Ide Center indefinitely and needed close care. My date's mother had befriended him in group therapy and, after checking with the staff, invited Truman to her house for Thanksgiving Day. My date said he was so proud of his mother for such a kind gesture.

He said he went to pick up Truman at the Center, a balding man, formerly a top-selling real estate agent, maybe fifty years old before his devastating heart attack. He wore a burnt-orange shirt and too-long dark slacks that caught at his heels. His necktie was wrenched to one side and flopped outside his plaid jacket. He had glassy eyes that wandered upward a lot, but when my date called Truman by name, Truman was perfectly polite and attentive, only his words hesitant:

"I'm. Very. Pleased. To meet you."

When Truman and my date arrived at his mother's house, she greeted them just inside the door.

"Doesn't Truman look handsome in his suit?' his mother said. 'He's bursting with fall colors."

Truman beamed with a kind of light my date admitted he did not quite grasp. He explained, Truman's look was not quite pride, but a kind of joyful clarity and relief my date had never seen before.

"I brought. A pumpkin pie," Truman said. "Frozen. I'll cook it."

And while my date and his mother fussed with setting their Thanksgiving table, Truman kept exclusive watch on his pie, an entire hour, until the buzzer sounded and he reached in the oven with bare hands, instantly burned them, and poured the unset filling down his front, luckily more landing on his shoes than scalding him through his jacket and shirt.

"Such a thing," my date said, "I'd expected. Anyway, we bandaged Truman's hands, cleaned him up, and proceeded to give thanks."

"That is a sad story, too," I said, fairly gawking at my date's exquisite fingertips, "but touching."

My date sunk back into his chair, concealing his delicate wrists once more. But his fingertips remained on the edge of the table. He was about to say something, make some new confidence, I was sure. There was something different about his hands. They'd become paw-like as he arched them at the precipice of white cloth, and I was almost frightened of his suit, those black stripes containing that strange charcoal night.

But then came our food. His walleye. My bigeye. I swear he waited until I nearly placed the first bite of bigeye in my mouth to say:

"There's more to the story."

He hadn't touched his walleye, and I was determined to ingest at least a couple forkfuls of my bigeye, and I did in anticipatory silence, all the while glancing out our window at bluish sedimentary layers of rock carved out by waves, a pile of eroded rubble below, half-submerged, lapped by the dark waters of Lake Erie.

All around, the chatter from other tables grew. Their voices echoed sharply from windowpanes. One was saying it was hard to find upscale restaurants right on the water anymore. Another was talking about this sauce or another on this entrée or another. The woman closest to me was arguing about substituting sliced tomatoes for the collard greens, nonplussed by the two-dollar upcharge.

When I relented at last, and said to my date, "Go on," his fingers advanced across the arctic white like two delicate cat paws, then stopped short of his blue goblet.

"We were halfway through our Thanksgiving dinner," my date said, "when my mother leaned to one side, kissed Truman on the mouth, and said to me, 'I love Truman and want to marry him.'"

I looked up from my bigeye and set my fork aside.

My date went on to say his mother'd only met Truman twice, and one of those times was at the very dinner they were eating. How could two such maimed people ever function together? He said he immediately ushered Truman out to his car, packed him inside, complete with pumpkin-stained suit coat, blistered and bandaged hands, and all the while his mother called through the front door screen:

"Don't take him away. I get so lonely. Please, let him stay!"

And Truman in chorus:

"Oh. Sorry. I spilled the pie. I ruined everything!"

It was then I realized I'd never had occasion to use the restroom at Pier W. This was the time. I excused myself, found the restroom, but before I went in, spotted an ancient diving suit on display, just outside, the entire visage leaning forward as if about to topple. The breastplate below the helmet read, "United States Navy Diving Helmet, Mark V." The bronze helmet had oxidized to deep brown and hung, pitched downward, at a sharp angle, staring at flat-toed lead boots, as if the diver were somehow penitent. Patches of tan cloth had fallen free from the rubber, and rubber-backed material was entirely gone from the sleeves and hands, as if jaggedly and cruelly amputated by time and wear. I'd never imagined anything could be worse than staring up at a dizzying skyscraper. When I left the Rapid Transit trains and walked to work, I kept my gaze straight ahead, sometimes down. Now, seeing the bedraggled and forgotten diving suit, I imagined myself at the bottom of Lake Erie, tethered to life by a slim hose, weighted by lead boots, so alone, looking up from below to feeble shafts of light. Looking upward! I blamed my date. His story of his mother and Truman had deep-sixed me. Why had he chosen *me* to tell it to? I felt like tearing for the surface and racing out of the restaurant. I wanted to climb back into my tower and phone the Dame, whom I'd not seen or spoken with in several months. I needed to tell her the story of Truman and his ill-fated bride, relieving me of its responsibility, ridding me of its drowning sorrows.

I washed up, and when I returned to our table, my date was into his walleye, saying how mild and flavorful it was.

"You were right," I said. "That is a sad story."

We ate in silence then. I halfheartedly dispatched my bigeye. He went about his walleye methodically, running the knife along the dorsal fin and teasing the meat out with a single tine of his fork. I started to think about after dinner, awkward stuff, to kiss or not, to suggest another date or not.

While he finished his walleye, I watched the city lights, their upside-down, distorted reflection on the lake water. Image and reflection each seemed half of a peculiar Rorschach shape, one luminous and clear, the other rippling and dark, each different, but an indivisible part of the other. Should the two ever be separated, the loneliness of a thing reflected, and its shivering reflection seemed unimaginable.

His poor mother! Poor Truman!

He set his fork aside, and again suckled at his wine glass, its stem pinched in his fragile fingers.

"That's not all," he said.

"You've got to be kidding."

This time, he crossed his arms over his chest, hiding his hands entirely.

"All right," I relented. "Tell me."

He leaned forward and laid one hand on the other in front of him, this time like two miniature nesting doves.

"Most of the way back to the Center," he said, "Truman kept saying he was sorry. I told him he couldn't possibly marry my mother. Truman said, 'I know,' and kept saying it even after I'd listed the many reasons why matrimony would be impractical for them."

As my date spoke, he was looking at the lake and brilliant bifurcated light, as if trying to see the same thing I'd seen in his story. Tragic loneliness. That's what I wanted to believe.

My date went on: he got Truman signed back in at the Center, said of course he felt awful, and so followed Truman to his room on the third floor for final departing condolences.

"I followed him, all the way to the door of his room," my date said, "awkwardly put my hand out to shake his gauze-wrapped paw, when a mournful howl arose the other side of his door, so sorrowful that Truman flung open the door, rushed to the bedside of his roommate, and fell to his knees, next to a man, a quadriplegic who strained his torso to right himself, as if to throw invisible hands about Truman's neck in a desperate, everlasting hug:

"'I'm sorry,' Truman said.

"'Oh, please, don't ever leave me again!' his roommate pleaded.

"'I promise,' Truman said and pulled the door closed."

The last thing my date heard through the door was Truman lying down on his bed.

At this point, the waiter came by, uttering his obligatory, "Will there be anything else?"

I wanted to say, "How could there be!"

When the waiter left, I propped my fist under my chin.

"Jesus Christ," I said. "That *is* the saddest story."

He blotted his lips with his napkin in his tiny hands and looked at the check. When he reached for his wallet, his Wonderland hands again disappeared.

"There's more."

"How on Earth can there be more?"

"Because it's only the saddest story I *tell*."

"Meaning there are others you don't tell? Because?"

"Because," he said and smiled, first I'd seen since meeting him, "I wouldn't want to self-disclose too much on a first date. How about a second one?"

* * *

FUCKER.

What sort of man tells a story like that? What made him think I'd fall for such a thing? A sadder story he never tells. Did he expect me to go out with him again, to beg him to hear it? I should have failed him in my class. I resolved to never see him or his Wonderland hands again.

Still, his ulterior motives aside, it was the sort of story that brought me out of my tower and across town that same weekend to see my parents in Shaker Heights, a surprise visit from their Zel.

It was early evening when I pulled into their drive—cold—and when I got out of my car, I pulled my faux fox tight about my neck. I was quick to rush to their front door before they could look out the picture window and see it was me. I pushed the door open, stood in the entryway, and beheld my mother, the Dame, her threadbare blue terrycloth robe, descending the stairs, hair slightly mussed on one side, yawning. I wanted desperately to run to her, fling my arms about her, take hold of her neck with my hands, bury my face in her mother-scent, hug her madly like I might the Madonna, my pinkie trigger finger stuck outward, quivering, pointing to some darker part of the house. I wanted her lobster hands, one claw supporting the nape of my neck, the other tapping at the small of my back.

But when she reached the foot of the stairs, she quickly stuffed her hands deep into the pockets of her robe. It stopped me. I got silent a few seconds, too long I was sure, the kind of silence I thought she might have felt was conspiratorial in some way.

"Where's Dad?" I asked.

"Out," she replied.

"Out where?"

"How should I know?" she said. "I see you've come down from your tower. What's up, Zel?"

I should have asked how her hands were, how she need not keep them from me, especially after my long and anticipatory ride clear across town for reassurance that there was a place I could always come to, if—well, just if.

I said, "Nothing," then, "oh, well, this guy I dated told me a really sad story."

"What about?"

"It's hard to explain."

"Well, try," she said, smiling, yet standing stiff, almost as if she was challenging me instead of inviting me inside the rest of the way.

"You know how someone tells a story a certain way, how no one can tell it the same way, and how after you hear a story like that you can never see anything the same way again?"

"What *is* this sad story?" she demanded, no longer smiling. "Just tell me."

"I don't think I can," I said. "I think he wanted another date in exchange for an even sadder story."

She looked at me skeptically a moment.

"Something sadder?" she said.

She shook her head, then without a word turned, walked upstairs, and left me alone in the doorway. I heard her bedsprings complain only a little as she lay back down. Above, I watched the light from her bedroom slant into the hallway, until I could no longer bear to look up there

ABOUT THE AUTHOR

Wendell Mayo (1953-2019) was a native of Corpus Christi, Texas. He authored five collections of short stories, recently, *Survival House* with SFASU Press in 2018. His other collections are *The Cucumber King of Kėdainiai*, winner of the Subito Press Award for Innovative Fiction; *Centaur of the North* (Arte Público Press), winner of the Aztlán Prize; *B. Horror and Other Stories* (Livingston Press); and a novel-in-stories, *In Lithuanian Wood* (White Pine Press). Over one-hundred of his short stories have appeared widely in magazines and anthologies, including *Yale Review, Harvard Review, Manoa, Missouri Review, Boulevard, New Letters, Threepenny Review, Indiana Review*, and *Chicago Review*. He received the National Endowment for the Arts Creative Writing Fellowship, a Fulbright to Lithuania (Vilnius University), two Individual Excellence Awards from the Ohio Arts Council, and a Master Fellowship from the Indiana Arts Commission. He taught fiction writing in the MFA/BFA programs at Bowling Green State University for over twenty years.

About the Press

Unsolicited Press was established in 2012 and is based in Portland, Oregon. The team produces poetry, fiction, and nonfiction by award-winning and emerging writers.

Learn more at www.unsolicitedpress.com.